The Journey

J. Adams

J. Adams

Published by Jewel of the West Publishing
West Point, UT

Copyright © 2008, 2012 J. Adams
Revised Edition 2012

ISBN # 978-0-615-20207-5

Library of Congress Control Number: 2008926617

To Ashley,
You are beautiful,
and you are loved.

Acknowledgments

There are so many people I need to thank for their help with this project. Fantasy is a genre I never thought I would attempt. I used to think that in order to write fantasy, your mind would have to be *way out there*, but I have since found that to be untrue. Imagination is everything, and believe me, mine has always run overtime. Maybe having eight children had something to do with that–I don't know. In any case, my *parental-induced* imaginings have finally produced something I am truly proud of–well, imaginings and some major divine intervention.

A big thanks to my friends, Christine Painter and Debbie Colledge for giving their time to read and edit for me. There's nothing like two extra sets of eyes. Thanks to Michele Bell for giving me so much encouragement, and a huge thanks to Josi Kilpack for helping me make a good story a great story. Thank you to my daughter, Seante' and my mother-in-law, Carol, for being my biggest fans and cheering me on. (No, of course they are not biased.) A special thanks to my husband, Sean, for always being there for me, and for supporting and believing in me.

Thanks to J. Scott Savage, James Dashner, Obert Skye, Brandon Mull, Brandon Sanderson, CS Lewis, J.R.R. Tolkien, and Christopher Paolini for being the royalty of fantasy and giving me joyous hours reading and something to aspire to.

And finally, a great big thank you to the youth for being my inspiration. I don't have to know your names to know you are amazing.

This is for you! May each of you *choose your path* wisely!

Detours on the path add new dimensions to the experience,
but some roads are better left untraveled.
Of course, in the end, the journey is as important as the
destination.

J.A.

Part One

Change Is Afoot

Zero

One Master

They say dreams are nothing more than your subconscious roaming free. But I know different. For me, dreams are a window to possibilities, things that can and will happen depending on actions. I see my dreams as clearly as if I am awake. It has always been this way with me. Even now, as I lay here, I watch the cast on the screen that is my mind, and I internalize everything.

The small room is lit by a single torch sticking out of a hole in the wall. The air is rank with the smell of old dirt, mingling with decaying bodies.

Three men stand chained to the stone wall, shivering

from the cold. With each deep exhale, large puffs of fog form in front of their faces, disintegrating quickly. All three men are blindfolded and stripped of their clothing. All are silent, for words will do them no good. They know what is coming and it would be both pointless and beneath them to beg. After all, they may possess a few evil virtues, but they still have their pride. They will not sink to groveling, not when their fate is set in stone. It always has been. They had just been too naive to realize how soon their demise would come. In some part of them there had even rested the thought that they had cheated fate.

"Any last words, gentlemen?"

The men remain silent as the familiar voice pierces through them. They know the voice well. They will take the sound of it to their graves.

"The time for multiple leaders is at an end," the voice continues. "There can only be one master now . . . and that, gentlemen, will be me."

Each man wrinkles his nose as the owner of the voice moves closer, the foul odor of his breath assaulting their senses. That is definitely one thing they will not miss.

The sound of the metal door opening followed by three new sets of footsteps makes the men stand a little straighter. Then they smile.

As the footsteps draw closer, the middle man opens his mouth for the first time since being confined and utters a single sentence that lingers in the silence of the room long after their decapitated heads fall to the floor.

"We will save a place for you in the underworld, my brother."

One

The Time Has Come

A gentle breeze stirs the lands and forests of Krisandor, the scent of pine and oak circulating through the warm air, adding a tantalizing sweetness that softly awakens the senses of a newly dawning day. Some would say the trees and the land of my home are as old as time itself. Though Krisandor was established just a little over a thousand years ago, the land has always been here.

The Krisandorians are a beautiful, peaceful people. We are governed, not ruled, by a peaceful king who loves us more than life itself. My people are industrious, producing all things in abundance, and prosperity abounds. Man loves his neighbor, there is no crime, no pride among us, and all citizens work for the common good.

Krisandor is a kingdom in which one longs to stay but inevitably has to leave for a time, for the peace and freedom of our beautiful kingdom has been hard won, and in order for us to truly appreciate the magnitude of sacrifice that keeps it thus, it is necessary to leave. In a word, Krisandor is safety, a kingdom that grants us a real sense of security, constancy, and love. A place where decency and fairness is a way of life. A place where integrity rules the whole heart.

From the palace grounds the laughter of children can be heard in the distance as they run and skip through the immaculate streets, giving chase between the elegant cottages. Their happy voices can be heard on the most distant shores, echoing like musical notes through the chambers of nature.

Inside the palace, I smile. There is nothing so joyful as the sound of a child's laughter. There is something magical about it. The sound speaks of innocence. I cling to that sound a moment longer, then I close my tear-filled emerald eyes and relish the feel of my father's warm and comforting embrace. The tone of his deep voice is soothing as he speaks words of love and comfort. Contemplating what I am about to face, I need those words now more than ever.

Keeping my head against his shoulder, I open my eyes

and take in the part of my room that is within my view. The whole bedroom, including the connecting sitting room, is decorated in lavender and white with gold fixtures throughout. The lace curtains cast shadow roses on the glistening white granite walls, and dainty winged figurines stand on various marble shelves lining the walls. The figurines are of Inchants. My father told me the Inchant people came to our kingdom over five hundred years ago because the peaceful home in which they lived on the other side of the world was dying away. One cannot help but marvel at the beauty of this graceful race of people. They now exist only in Krisandor and their purpose is to help where needed and bring joy to man and to themselves. They live as a community in the forest. One of my best friends, who is an Inchant, gave me the figurines and I cherish them.

Crystal dishes of dried orchid and jasmine petals sit on a white marble-topped dresser, and the scent fills the room with the sweetness of spring. *"A room fit for my daughter,"* I remember my father saying. How I love my room. I love my home and the warmth I feel here, and I relish the security of family.

The thought of leaving my home is both exciting and frightening. I have always been so settled, and my life so safe. But now the time has come for me to leave, to leave my home, my father, and every familiar thing I have ever known. It is now time for me to strike out on my own, to seek the new discoveries that await me.

I have always known this day would come and have prepared for it, for it is a step that must be taken. It is necessary. But now that the time is upon me, knowing I only have a few precious moments left with my father, I suddenly feel very unprepared for the world I will be going into. I am not ready for the change being wrought upon my life. Deep inside, I don't know if I will ever be ready. Does everyone feel this way? Has everyone who has made the journey been as afraid as I am? How can they not be? After all, the Krisandorians call the land beyond our kingdom The World With No Name. Who wouldn't be afraid of such a place?

I push the questions away and continue to cherish the feel of my father's large hand gently caressing my hair. It will be a long time before I am gifted that sensation again.

"I shall miss you so, Father."

My father, King Cillian, presses his dark, bearded cheek against my hair. "I will miss you, too, my angel, but the time truly will be short—shorter than you know. However, for you, it will seem long sometimes." He pulls back a little and looks into my eyes, and they match his own. "Just remember, my precious daughter, this journey is not only necessary but well worth the effort. It was for me, and everyone else who has taken it. You will be one of the final few to take this journey, for the season is coming to an end and change is upon our world." He falls silent and gazes out the window into the mountainous distance.

I see a different look of sadness cross his face and I know the reason. I know the look well. "You are thinking about Mother." It isn't a question. When he nods, I ask, "Will you never tell me why she is not with us?"

Father closes his eyes for a moment and heaves a deep sigh. "As I told you before, angel, she made her choice." He takes my face in his hands, caressing my golden skin. "One day the explanation will come. You will know it for yourself."

"Is it Mother's memory that keeps you from completely giving your heart to Maylee?"

"Maylee *does* have my heart," Father says wistfully. "She knows this. She also knows that until certain demons are put to rest, I cannot move forward. It will happen in time."

Sighing, my thoughts travel to the beautiful woman who has served in the palace and helped to care for me and my brother since we were small children. Though I often wonder about my birth mother, I love Maylee very much and have grown to think of her as my mother.

When Father says nothing else, I let the subject drop. I cannot help being curious about my mother, but I will not bring more pain to my father.

"How will I ever manage without you?" I whisper.

"You will," Father says with a smile. "I promise you, even though you will not be with me, I shall always be with you." He smooths the furrow in my brow with gentle fingers, smiling lovingly. "I shall be here waiting for you, but you will also carry me with you. Remember, your brother will soon come to be with you as well, so you will not be alone, even though it may seem like you are at times. Since he has already made the journey himself, his knowledge will be a strength to you."

I smile up at Father's loving face, then close my eyes as he presses a kiss to my forehead. Taking his hands in mine, I squeeze them, taing a deep breath. "I look forward to Sakriel's arrival," I say as my thoughts go to my brother. We have always been very close, and though we will only be separated for a short time, I will miss him terribly.

Nodding, Father stands, helping me up as well. I hold tightly to his hand as we walk down the brightly-lit, marble-tiled hall, lined with gilded mirrors and golden woven tapestries, before entering the enormous, glass-enclosed garden room in which we have spent so much time. The floral haven with its soft white sofas and chairs is my favorite place in the palace. The sanctuary exudes tranquility and calmness. If anyone is ever looking for me, they usually start with this room because I spend so much time here. It is here that I have spent a great deal of time pondering my life–pondering the changes that would inevitably have to be, and pondering the unknown future those changes will bring.

When we enter the room, Sakriel is waiting, his image mirroring our father's. He stands and I immediately move into his embrace, closing my burning eyes. It will be harder for me to say goodbye than I imagined. His fifty-year journey ended just three years ago and I hate being separated from him again.

"I shall miss you, little one," Sakriel whispers into my hair. "But I promise I will see you soon."

I smile. I am only three years younger than his one-hundred-five years, but he still calls me *little one*, and I love it. I finally draw back, looking from my brother to my father. "I love you both, and I will try to remember what you have taught me."

"We love you," Sakriel says, enclosing my hand between his large ones.

Father places an arm around my shoulders. "I have no

doubt you will have a successful journey." His eyes mist over. "Sometimes it will seem so long and things will come up that will make the road hard to travel, but you will make it, and you will be home again soon. You just need to remember who you are. You must remember your nobility."

Sakriel reaches out, taking my hand again. "And now, little one, it is time. Isiral is waiting outside to walk you to the gate."

My heart leaps and warmth spreads through me as thoughts of Isiral fill my mind. However, just as quickly, a deep sorrow rolls forth when I think of being separated from him. I know he also has to leave Krisandor one day to start his own journey, but will I really see him again? Though my heart yearns for it to be so, I cannot be sure, and this knowledge is very unsettling.

I tearfully embrace my brother once more, and then my father before turning to go. Though I know they are following me down the hall–I can hear the soft sound of their footsteps on the tiled floor–I force myself to stare straight ahead and not look back. I cannot *let* myself look back.

I will remember who I am, Father, I silently promise. *I will remember my nobility.*

When I reach the large white doors, I pause a few seconds before opening them. On the other side, Isiral is waiting with a handsome smile, and my own shy smile is automatic. He moves closer and I gaze up into his deep blue eyes, lifting my hand to touch a lock of blond hair that has escaped the silk tie holding the rest in place.

Isiral presses a warm hand to my cheek. "You are ready then?" His voice is thick with sadness.

I can only nod, unable to speak at the moment. Swallowing hard, I smile brightly. He takes my hand, placing it on his arm, covering it with his own. I lean into him as we begin our walk to the gate.

"Are you nervous?" Isiral asks me.

"A little." I heave a deep sigh. "Everything will be so different. I will not know anyone. And I shall miss Father and Sakriel."

Isiral's brow lifts slightly. "Only your father and Sakriel?"

I smile, squeezing his arm. "Oh, I suppose I shall miss you too." I try to keep my voice light, but falter in my effort. Unable to meet his eyes, I look away, saying nothing more.

We continue walking down the long stone walkway in silence. There is so much to say, so many things I long to tell Isiral, but I don't know how to begin or how to properly word what is in my heart. Occasionally, I glance up and find him looking at me, his deep blue eyes intent. A couple of times I notice he has even opened his mouth to say something but does not, and I wonder if he is struggling as much as I am.

"Ciran," a voice calls. I turn. It is my friend, Mazina. I watch the beautiful Inchant woman approach, the graceful creature's feet barely touching the ground as she walks. Her shoulder-length, golden hair is pulled up and away from her face, and her silky gold gown almost blends with the color of her skin. It billows around her slim frame. There are slits cut into the back, allowing unobstructed freedom for her shiny feathered wings.

Leaving Isiral's side, I go to her.

"I shall miss you, Mazina," I say, squeezing her hands.

"And I you."

"You and Ansel will most likely have several more additions to your family before I return."

Mazina laughs softly. "With a new pregnancy every ten years, unless my biological clock goes awry I am sure we will." She smiles tearfully. "And we will be sure to name one of the girls Ciran."

"But you already have."

"No matter," Mazina says, grinning. "You can never have too many Cirans."

My grin matches hers. As I look into the eyes of this beautiful being whose telepathic abilities are as strong as my own, our thoughts open to one another and I wonder how I can leave. How can I leave the people and the world that means so much to me? This life is all I have ever known.

All will be well, Ciran, comes Mazina's voice in my mind. *Let your mind and heart be at ease.*

The thoughts of comfort do calm me a little. My eyes drop to the graceful hands holding mine–hands that are strong enough to tear a limb from a body with next to no effort. Inchants are the most peaceful of people, yet if necessary, an Inchant's whole body can become a weapon. Their wings carry enough force to hurl an enemy a mile away. Their immortal bodies make them ageless. While the life expectancy of my own people is a little over two thousand years, Inchants will inhabit Krisandor long after its people are gone.

Smiling tearfully, I release her hands and we embrace.

"Come back soon, Ciran," Mazina whispers.

Closing my eyes, I nod, too overcome with emotion to speak. I know how uncertain everything will be. I draw back and we again hold hands tightly for a moment, and then we part. I watch my friend as she walks back toward the forest until I feel Isiral's hand on my shoulder. I turn and smile at him. He dries my tears with his gentle hands and we continue toward the gate.

When we finally reach the gate, I turn and gaze at the palace in the distance. The large white columns at the front entrance are both majestic and ominous. The blue sky is dotted with thick billowy clouds that hover over the high gray mountains. Streams of silver are woven through their fluffy peaks, providing the most beautiful backdrop for my home I have ever seen. I let my eyes drift to scan the immaculate courtyard of my home for a moment and take in the other numerous regal homes that fill the land. Several smaller walkways web from the various homes and meet the large one coming from the castle, which stretches to the main gate. The large doorway is the only entrance into Krisandor. I turn to Isiral as sudden tears fill my eyes.

"Promise me you will find me," I beg, taking the front of his robe in my hands. "Promise me."

Isiral pulls me into his arms, blinking back the tears filling his eyes. "I promise you, my love, I will find you. I have to find you." He draws back slightly to cup my face. "You are the only woman I would have by my side. You were chosen for me, and I for you." He kisses me softly, and then more deeply before releasing me and opening the gate.

I touch his face again, wiping a tear from his cheek. "My heart is yours," I softly say. "And I will try to be worthy of your love when we meet again."

Isiral says nothing more, but I see the feelings of his heart reflected in his gaze. I take a deep breath, and my smile is bright. Then I force myself to turn and walk through the gate, closing it behind me.

Isiral

A single tear slips down Isiral's face as he watches Ciran disappear through the gate, the breeze from the other side blowing her long, dark cascading locks back, as if they were being blown to him to allow him one more chance to sift his fingers through the soft strands. He hastily wipes his face and turns back toward the city, but his leaden feet will not move. His gaze moves back to the closed gate. The scrolled iron bars are covered in moss and violets. The beautiful collage of purple floral and greenery causes his heart to ache and prompts his mind to conjure up sweet visions of his beloved. His heart holds tightly to those visions and the feelings they invoke inside him. He will not let himself forget her. He *can't*.

Isiral has heard of a few people being gifted with some of their memories, or in some cases, all of them when they start their journey. Maybe he will be fortunate enough to be granted that gift as well. It would make it so much easier to find Ciran.

He sighs. *I will not forget. I will not!*

Even as he mentally shouts the emotional affirmation, deep down he knows what will be. What is necessary. But he is determined to find his way to her. He has to, because Krisandor, the Krisandor he knows and loves, would not be the same without her.

The sun is high in the sky now. Its rays peak through the clouds, falling brilliantly upon Isiral's shoulder-length blond locks, causing the billowing ponytail to shimmer like gold. He closes his eyes, raises his face toward the heavens, and smiles. It is almost time, and he is ready.

Yes, he will go on his journey. He will find her. And he will remember.

I know not where the path will take me, beloved, but I will remember.

And my heart will lead me to yours.

Cillian

Cillian presses his forehead against the cool glass of a

window in the garden room and closes his eyes. How he will miss his precious daughter, and how his heart aches for her, because he knows what her part will be in the coming events and what she will have to face. He understands what is to be. Her journey will not be as long as he had led her to believe.

He turns from the window as Sakriel approaches. When his son reaches his side, Cillian puts out his hand and his son takes it, tightening his own around it.

"Is she ready, Father? Will she be up to what will be placed before her?"

Sighing deeply, Cillian gives Sakriel's hand a reassuring squeeze. "She must be, my son. She must be." His heart tightens, the unrelenting pain growing more prominent with each passing second. "We have done all we can to prepare her, but it will still be difficult, as you already know. She will need you so much, son. So will others. The enemy's influence grows stronger with each passing day."

"I will do all that I can," Sakriel vows, looking into his father's eyes. "We will finish this, Father." He sighs, turning his gaze to the view of the land, taking in the beauty of his home. "We *must* finish it. Only then can the gate be barred and the way be permanently shut, so that complete peace can come."

Two
And So It Begins

As the first rays of morning sun shine through a glass section of the roof, warmth radiates around me as I sit in a chair opposite the smiling woman behind a beige marble desk. Every time we meet in Alana's office, I find myself taking in the woman's regal appearance. Today Alana is wearing a beautiful copper-colored silk robe, trimmed in teal green, a stark contrast to the beige robes I have been given. Her straight, chestnut-colored hair falls just below her shoulders and her smooth skin is a shade lighter than my own.

While Alana writes something down, I let my eyes scan

the now familiar room. The colors are neutral, but the crystal and brass chandelier and matching fixtures give the room an understated elegance. Framed paintings of floral arrangements adorn the walls and smaller ones rest on elegant brass stands and tables placed throughout the room. Exquisitely carved crystal figurines of various types of birds sit on six brass pedestals on both ends of the room. The windows, I notice, are all stained glass, making it impossible to see the beautiful trees I know line the gardens. My surroundings are quiet. Peaceful.

I have been a resident in the large, castle-like building for a month now, and other than my own name, I have no memory of my life before coming to this place. It is as if I just awakened last month and here I am. I have been feeling relatively calm in my surroundings, but now a subtle restlessness is beginning to fill me, like my soul is readying itself for a change.

I was told that this place is called the Place of Learning. It is here that I prepare for my journey, and the only knowledge I possess is what I have learned here. I was also told that while some people are gifted with memories of who they really are, as well as what their special purpose or task will be, most, like me, regain memories along their journey. I have had no interaction with anyone, nor have I seen anyone except Alana. Alana told me this is the way it is for everyone. It is the way things must be done.

Alana has been my instructor and has tutored me in many things. She taught me about Krisandor and its splendor. She has also been teaching me about who I really am. I find some of it hard to believe, but I still do my best to retain this knowledge, to hold on to the warm feelings it invokes inside me. Feelings of comfort and love, though I can't recall ever experiencing either before now.

A week ago Alana informed me of people, places and situations I may encounter in the world and has taught me the best way to handle them. She counseled me on choices and the ability to make the right ones. More importantly, she taught me what my purpose is for being here and the reward that will come should I successfully finish my journey. Always, Alana teaches with love and kindness.

Though the woman's words sound familiar to me, everything still seems so new, and I desperately hoped I will be able to retain the instruction I have received.

Alana stands and comes around the desk. She sits in a chair next to me. Taking my hand, she gives it a gentle squeeze. "The time has come, my dear, for you to begin. You are ready."

I look into her eyes, wariness seeping into me. I feel as

far from ready as I can be. "But what if I forget what you have taught me?"

"You will not forget. Not truly, as long as you earnestly strive to retain it." When I continue to silently look at her, my emotions unsure, Alana says, "I have only given you instruction. The only way you will truly be able to learn and gain real knowledge is by living through the experiences. Then, and only then, can you prove yourself worthy of your noble birthright and gain not only re-entrance into Krisandor, but you will also have what your heart truly desires most, and that knowledge will also come to you in time."

My brow furrows as I try to grasp what she is telling me.

She again squeezes my hand. "All right, simply put, your journey will be about choice. Just remember that every choice affects something or someone. Your very existence affects your surroundings. Your goal will be to change each thing you touch for the better. So always strive to choose wisely."

Comforted by her words, I smile. "Might I ask how long you have been here? You are so full of wisdom. Surely it has taken your whole life to learn these things."

"I have been here too many years to count."

"But you are so young."

Alana chuckles merrily. "No, my dear Ciran, I am not so

young. We are all older than we know, yourself included."

I look down at my own hands. They are as soft and smooth as the silk robe Alana is wearing. "I do not feel very old."

"Well, neither do I," Alana says with another chuckle. "Do not worry. Maturity will come with knowledge and with that, wisdom." She stands, urging me to stand as well. "Now, let us go and get you ready."

I swallow hard against my rising nervousness and nod. I stand and follow Alana out of the room and down the now familiar windowless hall. The walls are lined on both sides with paintings of a city. One painting seems to merge into the next, the focal point being the large palace in the midst of the other regal homes. I know without asking that this must be Krisandor. People of every size and color stand around the grounds in each painting. Children run happily to and fro, and each time I have stopped to study the paintings, I can almost hear their laughter. The artwork exudes peace and tranquility, and this fact fascinates me.

At the far end of the hall there is a brightly-lit room which houses an enormous gold plaque. On the plaque are all the names of people who have gone on their journey. The names are too tiny to read without a magnifying glass and there are too many to count. Across the room is an identical list of names, only this list is smaller. Each of these names has a tiny diamond next to it, for this particular plaque holds the names of the precious few who have completed their journey and returned to Krisandor. Looking at the difference in the returning number always brings a sadness to me that I cannot explain, and I hope with all my heart my name will be added to the returning list.

This is my final thought as I glance down the hall at the door one last time before entering my room.

I stand with Alana by the closed gate, marveling at how familiar it feels. Somewhere, sometime, I have stood at a gate similar to this one. At least I feel as if I have. My eyes move to the two large, dark-haired muscular guards standing on either side of the gate, each holding a spear with a sword strapped to his waist. Both look very strong and very good at their job. They smile at me and I smile back.

I smooth a hand down the front of the beautiful mauve and white robe I am wearing, and my other hand clutches a satchel filled with robes, gowns and other personal items that have been given to me. Heaving a deep sigh, I attempt to calm my nerves. I feel completely unready to leave, but I am determined to conquer my fear.

I watch Alana reach into her pocket and pull out a gold chain with a two inch long crystal attached. The light emanating from it is brilliant. My eyes widen when she unscrews the crystal from the base and pulls a small paper scroll from inside.

"What is it?" I ask her as she unrolls the small parchment.

"This is everything you will need to help you remember what you have been taught, and if you live by the words written here, you will not fail." She re-rolls the scroll, slips it back into the crystal, and reattaches the pendant. Slipping it over my head, Alana says, "The scroll was made to never tear and never fade. The words written here are as permanent as the paper. Take it out each morning when you awaken and each night before you close your eyes to sleep. Read what is written and engrave the words in your mind and heart. It is imperative that you do this. In these words you will find the strength to face anything that comes."

Alana pauses, her brow furrowing slightly. "A new season is upon us, Ciran, and changes are coming that will alter our very existence. You and many others will have a part in those changes." She squeezes my hand firmly. "No matter what you encounter, you must be strong and hold firm to these rules."

I can't help wondering at the sudden vehemence in her voice. Pulling my eyes away from her's, I lift the crystal and momentarily squints against the light it reflects. My eyes adjust and I smile. Though I am still nervous and a more than a little afraid of the unknown, I will be brave. I have to be.

"I promise," I finally say, my eyes again meeting Alana's. "I promise I will take the words into my heart. I shall do all I can to stay strong and be worthy."

She embraces me, her features softening. "I know you will, my darling girl," she whispers. "It will be hard, but I know you will. You and others like you are our future."

Three

A New World

My eyes widen in wonder as I take in the scene beyond the gate. There are people walking to and fro along the gray cobblestone streets. Small merchandising stands line the streets where people are purchasing various items. Large stone buildings loom imposingly, casting shadows over the stands, providing shade for both merchants and patrons.

I lift my eyes and gaze at the elegant structures. Some are more so than others, with stone spires reaching toward the heavens and archways that must have been created by the most gifted artisans. I guess this area to be the town square.

Glancing back the way I came, I am startled to find the

gate is no longer there. In its place is a large cluster of flowering bushes. Shades of pink, purple, and ivory burst from the branches, providing a feast of wonder and beauty to my eyes. Puzzled, I scan the area around the bushes, searching for the missing entrance. I see nothing but a wall of stone.

I should not be surprised, I muse with a half smile. There is definitely no changing my mind now. Not that I would even if I could. I am determined to see this through.

Turning back to face the crowded street, I open my satchel and pull out a small piece of paper. On it is an address Alana told me to find. There, I will find permanent lodging and work. Looking up and down the street, I stand unmoving for a moment, trying to decide which direction I should go. I close my eyes for a moment and attempt to shake away the sudden feeling of loneliness. Taking a deep breath, I draw forth the courage to forge ahead. I will get nowhere standing still as I am.

Just as I am about to step into the street, a black and gray carriage pulls up, stopping right in front of me, completely taking me by surprise. The carriage driver immediately jumps down and I am again startled, not only by his action, but his appearance as well. The man stands no more than four feet tall. Fiery red hair flows past his shoulders and bushy brows frame his gold-colored eyes. His smile is wide as he approaches.

"Are you needing a ride to Havenwood, miss?"

"I am," I reply.

"I am Orion. I am here to take you there."

"But . . . how did you know?"

"Why, we were expecting you." He opens the carriage door and holds out his hand. Sensing my hesitance, he says, "I will get you there safely, miss. You have my word."

I smile and nod. Taking Orion's offered hand, I step up into the roomy carriage. When he closes the door, I place my satchel on the seat and make myself comfortable. I let my eyes scan the inside of the carriage, awed by its immaculate luxurious splendor. From the crushed burgundy velvet adorning the walls and seats to the brass handles and trim on the doors, the carriage exudes elegance.

The carriage moves forward, the moving bodies in the square opening up a path as the driver steers the horses through the streets. Since I have never been around people, at least none that I can remember, I am fascinated by their diversity. Skin colors, clothing styles, hair styles, shapes and sizes, even their manner of walking is diverse. Something about each person I see stands out in my mind, and every face seems beautiful because they are all graced with a smile. A few people wave as I pass by and I wave back.

Within minutes we are out of the city and I take in the beauty of the vast countryside. The contrast is startling. A gentle breeze whips the tall grass in the open fields, and the high gray mountains provide the perfect backdrop, giving the land a wondrous look of enchantment. Lilies in an array of colors toil in the tall grass and dot the countryside, shimmering like precious gems. Birds dip and chase one another gracefully, the beautiful colors of their shiny feathers highlighted by the sun.

Up ahead is a forest and my anticipation grows. I listen to the clip-clop of the horses' hooves as we enter the colorful tree-lined section of the road. The scent of dogwood and wisteria seeps into my senses, making me suddenly long for a place I have no conscious knowledge of. Squirrels, chipmunks, and other inhabitants of the green paradise scurry here and there through the trees, the patter of their little feet on the crackling dried leaves providing proof of their busy existence and survival instincts.

As the carriage exits the forest, my gaze immediately falls upon the large building looming ahead. The massive, gray stone walls are covered in ivy and moss, the climbing green vines carpeting the building like a beautiful blanket. Flecks of sparkling stone shine through the green masterpiece, artistically created by nature. The numerous windows are paned with beveled glass and lined with colorful flower boxes.

The driver brings the carriage to a stop in front of a set of large wooden doors. Orion jumps down, immediately opening the carriage door.

"Here you are, miss," he says with a smile, his twinkling eyes dancing merrily.

I smile back, taking his offered hand. "Thank you very much, Mr. Orion, sir," I say, stepping down from the carriage.

"You are welcome. Now just go to the main desk and Fallon will take care of you."

Looking up at the large building, I turn back to Orion. "Sir, might I ask what this place is exactly?"

"It is a rooming place for people who are new to this kingdom–a place to work and live until they choose to move on. It is a safe place, a safe haven, hence the name Havenwood. There is another rooming place similar to this one on the other side of town, only it is called Fairmoor."

"But it is so beautiful. Why would anyone choose to leave?"

The small man sighs. "Some outgrow it. Some want to experience more than is found here. I am sure you will one day feel the same."

I doubt that. Thanking him again, I turn to go in.

"Oh, miss?" Orion says before I open the door.

"Yes?"

"Whenever you need my services, I am at your disposal, day or night."

"Thank you, Mr. Orion."

"You're welcome. And please call me Orion."

"Only if you call me Ciran." When Orion grins, I cannot help grinning in return.

"As you wish, Ciran." The small man bows and climbs back on the seat.

Orion

Orion ponders greatly on Havenwood's newest arrival as he rides away.

She is as beautiful and untouched as newly-fallen snow on an early winter countryside. She is innocent, unharmed, unspoiled, and without guile, the sight and scent of the first lavender and jasmine of spring, a thing of wonder and beauty that effortlessly claims the senses and makes one want to hold onto it for dear life.

But so were they all once, the small man mentally reasons.

Yet this one is different. He feels it deep in his soul. The purpose of her journey, her very existence, is fixed. Orion has witnessed the start of many a journey, has seen countless innocents corrupted by the things of man. Greed, pride, jealousy, vanity, and even by plain old curiosity. The weaknesses of man have swept away so many promising futures. He has seen it happen time and time again.

Orion presses a hand against his chest as his thoughts again travel to Ciran. He knows what will come. What must come. The beginning part of the journey is always so hard. It is hard on him, and those sent to his guided charge.

However, this fair maiden's pain is affecting him before it has even begun. He will know why that is soon enough.

He must prepare himself.

Twenty-five miles away in a deep, dark cavern in the mountains, a secret meeting is taking place. The leader of the group stands before the people, his dark, scaly body draped in a blood-red robe, illuminated by the firelight of torches sticking from crevices in the walls. All eyes are upon him, the faces holding various expressions of anxious and eager anticipation for the words they were about to hear. No one is paying attention to the screeching bats fluttering back and forth, casting shadows on the walls. Nor do they notice any of the small creeping inhabitants surrounding them. They are oblivious to the hooting of an owl on a tree limb just outside the cave, the howling of a pack of coyotes a hundred yards away, or the rattling of a snake coiled in a deep hole in a cave wall. It is as if these creatures have been drawn there as well. Still, nothing exists to those in attendance, except the figure standing before them. Their gazes are awe-filled, their very countenances immersed in an attitude of worship, and none dare to tear their gaze from him. They can't.

"The time is soon upon us," the dark figure says, lifting his hands and stretching them out to the group of men and women. His voice is gargled, yet powerful enough to resonate through the cave and hold everyone transfixed.

"War is coming, but do not fear, for our new kingdom is at hand and we will soon have what is ours. Together we will rule this world, and we will all share in the power that ruling will afford us." He pauses, letting his cold eyes slowly travel over the group. "My children. My brave sons and daughters. My brave and unstoppable warriors. It will take all of us to make this happen. We must stand strong and let nothing stop us. Only by standing together can we crush our enemy and bring him to his knees. He is weak, and he is nothing against us. In the end we are the ones who will rule. In the end we are guaranteed to be victorious. If we stand together, there is no way we can lose. All who are with me, say aye!"

As a chorus of ayes are shouted in unison, the leader smiles darkly, inwardly basking in the glory of his power. Success is within his reach. He can feel it deep in his bones, can taste it. He is a god to these people. His every wish is obeyed, his every command carried out without question or thought. He is life to them, the very air they breathe, the meat that sustains them, and he revels in it.

Closing his eyes, he takes a deep breath as he listens to the crowd chanting his name. Over and over again the sound swells in his ears, and oh, what a marvelous sound it is!

He *is* a god.

Yet he wants more. And soon he will have it.

Yes, everything is going according to plan.

Part Two
Valley Of Shadows

Four

Havenwood

Two years later.

As the sounds of morning softly filters into my room, I rub the sleep from my eyes and sit up. Lifting my arms, I stretch, and then get up and walk over to the bedroom window. Opening the beveled glass pane, I gaze out at the sunrise. Every morning starts this way and the view never changes. The interspersing colors of red, orange and yellow beckon my gaze, seeping into my soul, engraving a palate of beauty and wonder, which always begs for room in my mind's eye to savor throughout the day.

In the two years I have lived at Havenwood, I have truly come to love it here. My room is simple but beautiful. And cozy. The sunset-yellow tiled floor is covered with light green rugs and the yellow and green floral window coverings match the soft covers and sheets on the white iron bed. A large gold-framed painting of a grove of flowering trees by a stream hangs over the head of the bed. On my first night in the room, I had checked the hooks holding it in place for sturdiness because the thought of it falling on my head in the middle of the night would have made it impossible for me to sleep.

A white granite and wicker dresser holds my personal items, and my robes and gowns hang in a large matching cabinet. A crystal vase of flowers sits on the dresser, along with a silver brush, comb and mirror. A small stack of books sits beneath the bedside table. Other than these basic things, I haven't accumulated much else, but I have all I need. I am content.

After a few moments of watching the sunrise, I pull myself away from the window. Walking over to the dresser, I open the top drawer, smiling as I lift the crystal pendant from its cushioned spot, the light of it catching my eyes, producing a renewed wonder that I know will never fade. As is routine, I unscrew the crystal from its base and pull out the small scrolled parchment. I sit on the bed and read the words that are now etched in my memory and heart. The words of hope and love are my guidelines and bring me a feeling of renewed peace and joy. Not once have I missed a morning or night of reviewing the message Alana gave me, for it has become a precious gift to me, one with value beyond price.

Exercise kindness, for it is the gateway to unconditional love. And as you give it, you shall receive it.

He who possesses humility is teachable. Be teachable.

I love every principle of the scroll, but these are two of my favorites. Following several moments of meditation, I reroll the scroll, slip it back into the crystal, and return the pendant to its special place in my drawer. I then make my bed, put the room in order, and get ready for the day.

Having dressed, I check my reflection in the full-length mirror that stands in the corner. Tossing my long, dark braid over my shoulder, I tuck a couple of loose strands behind my ear. A few wisps of hair fall softly against my forehead, framing my face. I adjust the light brown cotton gown I wear for work and smooth a wrinkle on my shoulder. Feeling satisfied with my appearance, I slip my door key into the pocket of my gown and leave the room.

The spacious dining hall is already half full when I

emerge from the kitchen with another silver tray of sliced meats, cheeses, breads, vegetables, and a bowl of fruit.

Long wooden tables line the walls and round ones that seat six to eight guests are scattered throughout the dining area, casting shadows on the light gray stone floor where the sunlight shines through the windows.

The ivory colored stone walls are lined with large paintings of some of the most powerful men to ever reside at Havenwood. Their solemn faces stare out of the canvases. A few of the men boast hawk-like eyes that seem to pierce right through anyone casually glancing at the paintings. Two paintings in particular seem to command attention. One is of a man with long black hair and slanted eyes. A bulbous nose protrudes from his round face and there is a large mole on his chin. The other is of a gaunt faced man wearing round, wire-rimmed glasses that are half covered by shaggy brown hair that falls against his forehead. He also has a long scar on the right side of his nose.

For a while after I moved at Havenwood, I sometimes felt like the subjects of these two paintings in particular were watching me, and just entering the dining room used to make me shudder, but now I am used to the ominous faces peering from the walls and it doesn't disturb me anymore. Instead, I am curious about them. Who were they? What had the men done important enough to warrant the large portraits of them hanging at Havenwood? When I asked my coworkers I got various responses. Some thought the men were in important government positions. Others thought they were influential in the building of Havenwood, maybe even the builders themselves. No one knows for sure and I find that rather odd.

As I serve the customers, I am greeted with various smiles. I politely smile in return and chat for a moment with a couple of guests.

"And how is the fair Ciran this morning?" an older silver-haired gentleman asks as he normally does each morning.

"I am well. And you?"

"Now that I have been blessed with the sight of your lovely face this morning, I am well, too."

A blush heats my cheeks and I thank him for the compliment before returning to the kitchen.

My job is a rather simple one; take the prepared trays out to the guests and bring the empty ones back to the kitchen. For the other young women I work with, it is a monotonous task, but not for me. I enjoy meeting new customers, as well getting reacquainted with the old ones. This is the extent of my social life.

Occasionally, I walk across the road to a small shop to

purchase ink, paper, and a few personal items. The owner is always kind and very friendly. Her husband, though somewhat aloof at times, is congenial enough, but I haven't really gotten to know either of them well enough to consider them friends.

During my off hours I usually stay close to home, and I haven't really acquired any friends or acquaintances other than the people who work and live at Havenwood. For the most part, my life so far has been one of solitude.

But I have a feeling things are about to change.

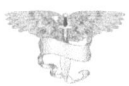

I am drying the last of the serving trays and placing them in a dark cupboard when my friend, Enya, enters the kitchen juggling five silver pitchers that had contained grape juice. I quickly take two of them from her overloaded arms.

"Thank you," Enya says, her cheeks flushed. "For a moment I wondered if I would make it in here without covering myself in purple."

"It seems you have expanded your talents," I say with a chuckle.

"I have had a lot of practice." Her blond locks tumble over her shoulders, having escaped the loose bun at the back of her head.

We take the pitchers to the back of the kitchen and clean them. Once they are dried and polished, I help Enya put them away.

As Enya leans down to put the pitchers in the lower cupboard, some of her hair falls to one side, exposing a patch of dark scaly skin on the back of her neck. It almost looks like a snake skin pattern or some other form of reptile. I am finding this is common among many of the people I meet daily, and figure it must be some sort of ailment or skin condition. For some, it seems the condition is worse than others. Not wanting to offend anyone, I have never inquired about it. It doesn't seem to bother those who have it, so I try not to give it much thought. But whatever it is must not be contagious because I have been at Havenwood for two years and haven't caught anything yet.

"Do you have plans for this evening?" Enya asks, standing up and stretching her arms.

"Not really. Orion agreed to lend me another book. I thought I might do a little reading."

Enya sighs. "You are always either reading or keeping company with Orion, Ciran. You never get out and have any fun."

I smile. "Reading *is* fun. I enjoy expanding my mind and

making new discoveries. *And* I enjoy my visits with Orion. He is very entertaining."

"Well, since you like expanding your mind and being entertained, I have just the thing for you. Kundar is hosting a party tonight. Come with me."

"Thank you, but I think I am going to stay in tonight."

"Oh, come on, Ciran," she whines. "You stay in every night. This will be fun. And besides, Kundar has someone he would like you to meet."

I shake my head, sighing, a slight smile tugging at the corners of my mouth. "Do you two ever tire of trying to be matchmakers?"

"Of course not," Enya replies with a sly smile. "We want everyone to be as happy as we are. There is someone for everyone, you know. Please say you will come."

"Maybe," I finally say, relenting a little. "I will think about it."

"Oh, don't do that or you won't come." Enya points a finger at me. "I know you, my friend. You will talk yourself out of coming if you think long enough."

I release a low snort. Enya knows me well. Maybe I should go. I have been at Havenwood for two years and have yet to step out of my comfort zone. It is time for me to get out a little and expand my horizons. I really don't have a life outside of my work and Havenwood. Truthfully, the only friends I have are Enya, Kundar, Orion, and a couple of the girls in the kitchen who work the morning shift. I have never ventured anywhere else because I feel so settled at Havenwood. I feel safe.

How will I ever grow if I never leave the safety of my surroundings to seek the experiences that will bring that progression about? After all, isn't that why I am here?

Deep down, I know why I have never ventured anywhere; because of the returning name plaque at the Place of Learning. I don't want my name to be left off that plaque as so many others are. True, I still have no memories of the home I will be returning to, but I want to complete the journey just the same. I want to go back. Still, I cannot stay as I am now, naive to the things of the world. I cannot waste away my years this way.

I am suddenly a little frustrated with myself for waiting so long. I have been here for two long years! Waiting for what? For a sign to suddenly drop from the sky, letting me know it is time to do something with my life? Am I supposed to suddenly know when to take a chance and truly begin to live? There are no guarantees, no certainties, and there is no crystal ball to tell me what will happen in my life. I have choices. They have always been here before me, waiting to be made.

After mulling over these thoughts another moment I say, "All right, I will come."

"Wonderful!" Enya cries. "You are going to have a good time. I promise."

"I am holding you to that," I tell her, grinning at her excitement. "But do not be disappointed if nothing comes of the introduction to your friend."

"I will not, as long as you promise to stay open to the possibility. After all, he just might be the prince you are waiting for."

"Or the frog I want to avoid."

Enya laughs heartily. "That may be true, but I very much doubt that. I think you will be quite pleased."

"Hmmm, now I am intrigued," I say, genuinely looking forward to the evening.

Later, during a leisurely moment, I slowly stroll through one of the dimly lit corridors of Havenwood and study some of the paintings hanging on the walls. There are various pieces of artwork placed on wooden pedestals here and there–wooden and stone figures of large birds and forest critters whose faces don't look quite normal to me. With their enlarged eyes and exposed teeth, they look a little frightening.

After a few moments of studying the various pieces of art, I find myself standing in front of a life-size statue of a robed man holding a bowl of grapes in one hand, his other hand outstretched with a small bunch of fruit in an attitude of offering. The statue is made of white marble, etched in meticulous detail.

The face is handsome and kind, yet almost deceptive, as if he knows some great secret. The life-like eyes give me a sense of eeriness as they almost seem to follow my every move, as if he is saying to me, *Yes, I can see you. Do not let this body of stone fool you.*

Shivering, I rub the goosebumps on my arms. This is a hallway of Havenwood I have never ventured into before. I have never desired to until today. Maybe the conversation with Enya this morning has opened a vein of adventure in me. I can't help wondering who the model was and why this particular piece of art is placed with all the other hideous pieces lining the walls.

A sudden coldness sweeps through the corridor, taking me by surprise. Casting one more glance at the statue, I turn and head back to my room.

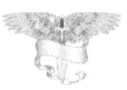

Hearing a knock at the door, I open it and am greeted by Orion's cheerful smile.

"Another book for the fair Ciran," he says, holding a thick novel out to me.

"Why thank you, kind sir. I shall read it and return it in a couple of days."

"Take your time. I am in no hurry to get it back."

"You are always so good to me," I tell him, reaching down and affectionately touching his shoulder.

"Always," he agrees softly. His eyes roam over the dark teal and gold robe I am wearing and his brow furrows slightly. "Going out this evening?"

"Yes," I answer, giving him a wide smile. "Enya is taking me to a party at Kundar's estate."

"I see," he says, sighing deeply. "This will be your first time venturing over to Darkton, will it not?" His voice is soft.

"It will be my first time venturing anywhere," I answer, wondering at the seriousness of Orion's expression. "Is something wrong?" I ask, again touching his shoulder.

Orion looked up into my eyes, his golden gaze soft but intent. "I know you have been here for some time now, but you are still at the beginning of your journey and I am concerned for you."

"I will be fine, Orion. Besides, I have to start expanding my horizons sometime. Kundar's party is as good a start as any."

"You speak the truth, however, I must caution you. You will meet many people tonight. People who are not what they seem. Just remember who you are, fair Ciran, and why you are here. Do not forget even for a moment." He takes my hand, squeezing it, his fiery red hair shimmering in the light of the chandelier in the hallway. "Do not forget even for a moment."

I nod, unable to understand why Orion is so serious. Is it wrong for me to venture out now? In two years I have hardly left the grounds. Now I yearn to do so. I *need* to do this. After all, it is just a party, and I trust Enya and Kundar to look after me. I will be fine.

"I will not forget," I finally say. "Everything will be fine." I move to close the door.

"One more thing," Orion says quickly. "There is a very popular drink many people indulge in. It is called Splendorfire."

"Really? I have never heard of it."

"No, you would not have. The drink is not served here at

Havenwood. Once upon a time it was, but there is a reason it is no longer here. You see, the drink is not good. It changes people and causes them to do things they would not otherwise do. It produces a weakness in them. And on the indulgence of Splendorfire rest all other weakness that are sure to follow. Please remember this if, or when, it is ever offered to you."

"It sounds terrible," I say. "Why would people choose to indulge in something that would weaken them?" Even as I say this, my thoughts wander to the return plaque in the Place of Learning. "Is that why so many people do not return to Krisandor?"

"In a way," Orion answers, seeming pleased that I remember the plaque. "However, people can change should they choose to."

Risk not returning to Krisandor? This is definitely not something I want to happen to me. I look into Orion's eyes, my resolve firm. "Thank you for the warning. I will heed your counsel."

Orion

Orion watches from his bedroom window as Ciran and

Enya disappear inside Kundar's personal carriage. Ciran's black hair shimmers in the moonlight and he is once again struck by her beauty. He keeps his gaze fixed on the carriage until it is but a dot in the distance. How this young woman has ingrained herself in his heart so, he doesn't know. Perhaps it is because in the time since she arrived, he has learned who she is, what her purpose is, and why the outcome of her journey is so important.

Ciran's father had been a true friend to Orion before Orion left Krisandor over two hundred years ago—one of the truest friends he has ever known. For Orion, it is as if he is letting his own daughter step into an abyss of darkness with only a dim light to guide her way. He is powerless to stop what will be, and powerless to tell her what is to come. Even if he could, he knows he wouldn't. He could never take the coming experiences away from her, for to do so would deprive her of the growth and the knowledge she will surely gain from them.

He looks up toward the heavens, gazing at the dark sky, taking in the celestial scene before him.

The stars are beginning to align, and the land grows restless. Orion listens to the groaning of the land shifting around him. He has noticed during his daily travels that trees are slowly beginning to die here and there. Smooth places on the ground are becoming rough. The forests are not as plentiful as they once were, and some of them are even devoid of wildlife now. The days are growing shorter. The warm springtime temperatures that have always been so perfect are now going through the most erratic changes he has ever seen. On one day the heat is almost unbearable, the next it is absolutely freezing. The land is still beautiful, but the elements are completely unpredictable.

All are signs of the spreading evil.

His thoughts return to Ciran and he is freshly overwhelmed by her beautiful and unspoiled innocence. Heaving a deep, sorrow-filled sigh, he closes his eyes and presses his forehead against the cool glass, his hands forming fists as a pained whisper escapes his lips.

"It has begun, Cillian. Her test has finally begun."

Five

Ubal

Joyfully scanning the large crowd, I join the rest of the guests in applause as a colorfully dressed Kundar takes a final bow, having ended another of his brilliant one-man performances of a satirical comedy that was actually written for several players. I laugh as Enya rushes up on the stage and kisses him before he can come down. Kundar sweeps her up in his arms, swinging her around. He is so tall and easily lifts Enya's small frame off the ground. Studying his dark good looks and Enya's beautiful features, I find them to be a striking couple. One cannot help noticing the large scaly patch of skin just below Kundar's chin when first meeting him, but now I hardly notice it at all.

However, as I sit in the great hall filled with people showing varying degrees of the same skin condition, some far worse than others, I almost feel like *I* am the different one, and it makes me feel slightly out of place. I momentarily wonder what others think of me.

Enya finally joins me at the table. "Are you enjoying yourself?" she asks, taking a sip of her drink.

I hesitate a moment, feeling a renewed concern for my friend over her choice of drinks. From the moment we arrived, I have watched Enya and Kundar consume several goblets of Splendorfire and my concern for them has increased. But Enya seems okay and Kundar looks to be in control. "I am enjoying myself very much," I finally answer with a forced smile, clearing the previous thoughts from my mind. "Kundar is very entertaining."

"He is magnificent, is he not?" Enya boasts with loving pride and I chuckle.

"Yes, he is." I watch Enya staring across the large hall at Kundar where he stands talking with another gentleman. When Kundar smiles our way and heads to our table with the man, Enya's face lights up even more. I am overjoyed for my friend's happiness. I have never seen two people more in love. I grin as Enya sighs with delight. Then I glance at the man walking by Kundar's side and I am immediately struck by his attractiveness.

The man is of average height and medium build. His brown hair falls to his shoulders and his gray eyes are striking. As he comes closer, his face is familiar to me. I could almost believe I have seen him before, but I know that is impossible. I would definitely remember. When he smiles at me I smile back, and a blush heats my cheeks.

"Hello, my darling," Kundar says, leaning down and kissing Enya. He then smiles at me and gestures to his friend. "Ciran, I would like you to meet my good friend, Ubal. Ubal, this is Ciran."

"It is indeed a pleasure," Ubal says, taking my hand, squeezing it gently.

"It is a pleasure to meet you as well." I am briefly startled by the unexpected coldness of his hand.

"I have known Ubal for a long time," Kundar tells me, placing a hand on his friend's shoulder. "He is indeed a good friend to all."

Ubal smiles, thanking him for his kind words.

Kundar takes his seat next to Enya, drawing her close, and the two are immediately wrapped up in each other.

Ubal sits in the chair next to me. I watch him take in the half empty glass goblets before requesting another round of drinks for everyone. He looks at the clear liquid in my glass. "Water?" he states with slightly raised brows. "Surely you would like something a little stronger than that. Perhaps some Splendorfire?"

"No," I quickly assure him. "Water is fine."

Ubal glances over at Kundar and Enya as they drain their goblets before moving his eyes back to me. "Water it is, then." He nods to the server, and then smiles, leaning back in his chair. "So Kundar tells me this is your first time away from Havenwood."

"It is," I say.

"It is her first time anywhere," Enya says. When I shoot her an embarrassed scowl, she smiles sweetly.

"Are you enjoying your time in Darkton, then?" Ubal asks, looking at me intently.

"Yes, I am. I have enjoyed getting out and meeting others."

"Well, I for one am definitely glad you came. I have heard a lot about you from Kundar and have been looking forward to meeting you. I must say, you are definitely as beautiful as I've been told."

"Thank you." Heat flows into my cheeks. Though I am flattered, I am not used to such compliments. I glance over at Enya and she winks.

"It looks like another successful party tonight, Kundar," Ubal says as his eyes slowly move around the crowded hall. He casually rests his hand on the back of my chair.

"It is only filled to the rafters because the people knew you would be here."

"I am no one special," Ubal says, his voice laced with humility.

Kundar grins. "You know I speak the truth, my friend. Just look around you."

My eyes follow Ubal's around the hall, and truly, over half the guests in attendance have their gazes fixed on our table. I turn back to him. "It does seem that you are the center of attention."

Ubal chuckles. "Am I?" His eyes dance merrily.

I shyly look away, taking a sip from my goblet. Ubal is a charming man. As he and Kundar talk, I let my eyes briefly roam over his person. His brown hair is brushed to a sheen that reflects the flickering lights of the hall. His black and red velvet robe is a work of art and hangs on him like it is artistically draped, so perfectly placed each crease is. His fingers are manicured, and the gold ring he wears on his right hand is studded with small rubies and stands out against his fair skin. He looks to be a man of no small fortune or reputation.

After a while the music changes and more people begin to rise from their seats and move to the dance floor. Glancing at Ubal, I meet his intent stare.

"Dance with me," he says, immediately standing, holding a hand out to me.

"I do not know how," I tell him, looking away shyly.

"It is not very hard at all, Ciran. You need only follow my lead." He wiggles his long fingers, indicating that he won't take no for an answer.

Raising my eyes to his, I smile and timidly place my hand in his, again surprised by its coldness. He leads out to the dance floor, and I am unsettled by the numerous gazes shifting toward us. Following Ubal's instructions I place my hand on his shoulder. Ubal takes my other hand in his and wraps an arm around my waist. A sense of nervousness enters me. I have never been this close to a man, at least not that I can remember. As Ubal begins to lead me slowly, I release a deep breath, not realizing until this moment that I have been holding it. Hearing him chuckle, I look up at his face, and his mouth turns up in a wide smile that I again find charming.

"Now that you are breathing again, may I assume that my efforts to put you at ease are starting to take effect?" His voice is teasing.

"You may," I answer.

Ubal chuckles again and guides me to the middle of the floor, the sea of coupled bodies parting as we slowly and smoothly passed.

I glance around us, meeting the smiles and stares directed at us. "You truly are popular, aren't you?"

Ubal shakes his head. "Did it ever occur to you that it may well be *you* who is garnering all the attention. Not many ladies in the land are gifted with, or even rival your beauty." He smiles, looking into my eyes. "You captured my eye the moment you walked in tonight. Perhaps others cannot pull their eyes away either."

"Thank you," I said softly, looking away as my cheeks warm.

"I only speak the truth, fair Ciran. I only speak the truth. So tell me, how do you spend your free time?"

"Well, I read a lot."

He smiles. "I am addicted to reading as well. Knowledge truly is power, and is that not what we all desire?"

"I don't know if I agree."

His expression is one of thoughtful surety. "Do you desire to master yourself?"

I am perplexed by his question. "I am not sure what you mean."

"Well, do you wish to have complete control of your thoughts, feelings and actions?"

"Yes," I answer.

"Then you quest for power, for mastery of ones self *is* power. Do you not agree?"

I smile. "It is. I guess I have never thought of it in that way."

His smile widens. "Then I think it will be my job, fair Ciran, to open your eyes–a position for which I would be happy and most honored to fill." When I shyly lower my eyes, he adds, "You know, if it is possible, I think you are even more beautiful when you are blushing. In time I hope to be able to hold your eyes with mine through the warming of your cheeks."

Challenged, she bravely raised her eyes to his again. "How is that?"

"Much better," he says, chuckling softly. "A very good beginning indeed."

I spend the rest of the evening with Ubal, laughing and talking in between dances. Throughout the evening I sense that numerous men in attendance want to dance with me but dare not ask because I am with Ubal. It seems no man has the nerve to even approach. It is as if there is an unspoken agreement around the hall that no one is to cut in on Ubal.

At the night's end, Ubal walks me out to Kundar's carriage. Enya is staying a little later and says she will be along in a while.

"It has been a pleasure," Ubal says, raising my hand to his lips.

"It has been," I agree, grateful for the darkness that shrouds my face. I am sure it is beet red at the moment.

"May I call on you tomorrow?"

"You may," I answer, my voice demure.

Ubal sighs, helping me into the carriage. He squeezes my hand through the carriage window. "Until tomorrow, fair Ciran." I nod and he steps back as the driver steers the carriage away.

Ubal stands in the same spot until Ciran's carriage is no longer visible. He continues to smile as Kundar silently appears at his side.

"It was a good night," Kundar comments, looking into the distance.

Ubal nods. "Truer words were never spoken, my friend. It was a good night indeed."

Later, Enya stands behind Kundar's chair and firmly massages his shoulders, loosening the tight knots in his muscles.

"The night was wonderful," she says with a sigh. "And Ubal looked very pleased. I know Ciran was."

"He was," Kundar agrees. "Strange though," he muses. "Of all the women constantly surrounding him, Ciran is the first one he has shown any interest in at all, yet it seems to go even deeper than that. Hmmm."

"What exactly does "hmmm" mean?" She pauses in her ministrations, wondering what Kundar was thinking.

"It means there has to be more to this. I cannot help but wonder . . ."

"Wonder what?" she presses.

"Nothing, my dear. You know me and my overactive imagination."

"Well," Enya says, leaning down and kissing his ear, "What matters is that we have done what we set out to do. Our job is finished and we have brought together two lonely people. Ciran was so taken with Ubal, I am sure she will be exclusively his within a week."

"Perhaps." He reaches for Enya's hand, pulling her in front of him and onto his lap. "Now, my lovely, let us forget about Ciran and Ubal. Must you really leave tonight?"

"I suppose not," she answers, smiling seductively.

"Precisely what I wanted to hear."

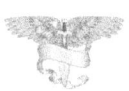

Orion

Sighing with relief, Orion meets Ciran's carriage as the driver pulls up in front of the large doors. Ciran smiles when she sees him.

"This is a surprise," she says as he takes her hand, helping her down.

"I just wanted to make sure you arrived safely before I retired for the night."

"I appreciate your thoughtfulness," she says, giving his hand a gentle squeeze.

"How was your evening?"

"It was wonderful. I cannot remember enjoying myself more."

"Shall we sit a moment?" Orion gestures to a granite bench a few feet away.

"All right."

The two make themselves comfortable and silently stare up at the stars for a few moments before Orion speaks. He had needed a moment to gather his thoughts. He senses with amusement that Ciran is bursting with excitement to share her experiences of the night.

"Tell me about your evening."

Ciran sighs, releasing a delighted giggle. "Oh, Orion, I wish you had been there. The music, the food, the entertainment–everything was simply wonderful! The people were beautifully dressed and everyone was so nice."

Orion fights the furrowing of his brow and holds a smile on his face. "Was there anyone in particular who garnered your attentions?"

Ciran looks at him, her eyes showing surprise. "Indeed there was. But how did you know?"

"I just assumed a young woman with your beauty would not last through the night without someone favoring her with his attentions."

"You assume correctly," Ciran says shyly.

"Might I inquire the gentleman's name?"

Ciran nods and Orion can see the excitement in her eyes. He attempts to school his features without success.

"His name is Ubal and he . . ." She pauses. "Do you know him?"

"I know *of* him. He is a very popular figure, and very well known throughout the land."

Ciran grins. "After witnessing the attention he drew at the party tonight, I must say I agree. I enjoyed his company very much."

Orion heaves a small sigh, squeezing her hand gently. "Please be careful, fair Ciran," he cautions her. "I know you are eager to embrace all that life has to offer, but just remember that unseen evil abounds around us. It grows by the day and can come from anywhere." He presses a hand to her cheek. "Take care that it does not touch you."

"What do you mean?" she asks, her expression suddenly perplexed. "What does that have to do with Ubal?"

Orion closes his eyes, shaking his head slightly, knowing he can't say more. Not now. Not yet. It isn't his place. He has been sworn to secrecy and he will keep that vow, no matter how much it pains him to do so. She will need to make some discoveries on her own.

Opening his eyes, he smiles. "Do not mind me, I tend to worry too much. You are like my own daughter. You are a strong young woman, Ciran, and you will grow even stronger with time. Of this I am certain. Know that I am always here for you. Will you remember that?"

Her expression is still one of worry. "I will remember."

Orion's face quickly brightens, drawing a smile from the young woman. "All right, now tell me more about your evening."

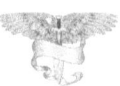

I am completely exhausted by the time I reach my room, yet I cannot stop smiling. It has been an amazing night! I'd had more fun than I dreamed I would, and I eagerly look forward to seeing Ubal again.

Foregoing my nightly study of the scroll–I promise myself I will make it up tomorrow–I quickly change and get into bed. Closing my eyes, I take a few moments to review the events of the night before drifting into a restful slumber.

The next afternoon finds me picnicking with Ubal beneath a large tree on the grounds of Havenwood. The afternoon weather started out mild but now it seems restless, as if a pending rainstorm is on the rise, yet the skies are still clear, contradicting the feeling in the air. A family of ducks waddle around the bank of a small pond a few yards away. They look in our direction but never come near despite the food I place out for them. The intermittent croaking of a frog is very soothing. A moment later it's voice is joined by another.

Gazing at my surroundings, I cannot help thinking about last night and how much I enjoyed myself. Ubal had been witty with a sense of humor that was completely engaging. I could definitely see why he was so popular, and garnering his attention for the whole evening had made me feel special, and envied.

I smile and pass Ubal a plate of sliced roast beef, cheese, and bread. "What are you normally doing during this time of day?" I ask him before taking a bite of my food.

"Oh, this and that," he answers casually. "Most of the time, just like yourself, my nose is stuck in a book."

I can definitely believe that because he seems so learned and well versed. "What kinds of books do you read?"

"Mostly fiction and philosophy. There are so many great works out there. I devour as many of them as I can. And what about you?"

"I love poetry, plays, and anything that I can gain useful knowledge from."

"Hmmm," Ubal responds, his tone thoughtful.

Taking an apple from the basket, I bite into it, chewing for a moment. "Do you work?"

"Only when I choose to." He smiles. "Being wealthy has its privileges. I do what I want, when I want."

I quietly ponder on this a moment. "You are fortunate to

have such freedom."

"I am," he agrees. "But mine is a lonely life. True, I have many friends and acquaintances, but . . . there are still those times when I need more." He pauses, looking at me intently. "Today is a good day because I am spending it with you."

A unexplainable feeling of wariness enters me, but I quickly brush it aside and meet his steady gaze with my own, captivated anew by his charms. "The feeling is mutual."

As the days and weeks pass, I spend many of my free evenings with Ubal. When I am with him, there is never a dull moment. I find him full of life and laughter, and I gain new experiences and feelings every second I am with him. We share our opinions and views on books, plays, and poetry. We spend hours just discussing our feelings and views on life.

Finding it easier with each passing day to brush aside the slight feeling of uncertainty I had initially felt when I was with him, I embrace the changes now coming over me. I catch the visions his ideas invoke in me and savor the carefree moments. My initial hesitance of traveling into the unknown has all but vanished, along with Orion's occasional counsels of caution. Ubal has introduced me to a whole new world. A world full of mystery and excitement. A world of unlimited possibilities. It is his world and I revel in it. For the moment, I am happy.

Cillian

As the Krisandor sun begins to set between the gray mountain peaks, Cillian kneels on the cold tile floor, pressing his face against an arm of the white sofa. Against his will, tears seep from his closed eyes, wetting the spotless material. A breeze softly blows through an open window and gently stirs the hanging collage of crystals, catching the fading light. The beautiful music they play is soft and low, but Cillian is oblivious to it.

He can physically feel the agony of the choice his daughter is about to make, and the pain of it threatens to tear his heart in two. At the same time, he has to force himself to swallow back the anger rising inside of him. It begins to swell against his insides, making it hard to focus his thoughts.

Anger is not the way. He knows this. But Ciran is his child, his own flesh and blood, and as much as it hurts, he must stay his hand. He cannot help her. All he can do is try to send her comfort. It is taking all of his strength not to give in to his desperate urge to reach inside her thoughts and steer her clear of the path she is stepping onto. He wants to shelter her from the storm. But alas, he knows he cannot. She must make it through this small stretch of the journey on her own. And he knows she will. She is strong, stronger than even *she* knows. That strength will shine in the end. Of this, he is certain.

"All will one day be set right, my angel," he whispers through the tears. "All will be set right."

"Father." Sakriel's deep voice cuts through the silence. He quickly moves to his father's side. "What is it?"

Cillian slowly stands, meeting his son's eyes, an immediate look of determination creasing his brow. Drying his face, he places a firm hand on Sakriel's shoulder. "The first strike has been made, my son. The enemy is playing on your sister's emotions and is moving faster than we anticipated. We must ready ourselves. *You* must get ready. She will need you soon."

Six

A Well-Worn Path

Smoothing my hands down the gold-trimmed, rust-colored robe, I examine my reflection in the mirror. The robe is a gift from Ubal. He presented it to me yesterday and asked me to wear it tonight because he has a special evening planned. When I told him he didn't need to give me such an extravagant gift, he said he wanted to give me something that equaled my beauty, and because he couldn't find anything, the robe would have to do. I smiled, kissing his cool cheek.

Satisfied with my appearance, I walk over to the window and gaze out across the shimmering green land, my eyes taking in the mountainous backdrop. The view causes my mind to drift to a distant memory of another view even more glorious than this one, a scene I sense took my very breath away. But just like the other times, the flash of memory comes and goes in the blink of an eye and my mind cannot seem to retain it.

Just as I begin to ponder on the memory there is a knock at the door.

Thinking it is Ubal, I hurry to the door. I open it and find Orion staring up at me. My smile fades slightly. I am a little disappointed, but not unhappy to see Orion. I take in his appearance. The cream-colored, silver-trimmed robe he wears sets off his fiery red hair, making his countenance almost glow. I have never seen him dressed in such regal looking attire.

"Going out again, are you, miss?"

"Yes," I answer, my smile returning. "I dare say you are as well. You look wonderful."

"Thank you."

He quietly stands unmoving, a sudden furrow creasing his bushy brow. "Is something wrong?" I ask him.

Orion hesitates, the twinkle absent from his eyes. "Do not go tonight, Ciran."

A perplexed furrow creases my own brow. "Why ever not?"

He reaches out, taking my hand in his. "It would not be wise."

"Why?" I ask again, wondering why he is so concerned about how I spend my free time. Orion has always been here for me and he is a good friend. I respect him a great deal, but I cannot understand his worry for me. Nothing scandalous has happened. I always try to do what I am supposed to, and I have always listened to his counsel, despite sometimes feeling that he treats me like a child.

"I will be with Ubal, Orion. Why should I not go out with him?" I sigh, sudden frustration growing in me. "Why are you always so concerned about me being with him?"

The small man takes a deep breath. "Ciran," he says softly, "you do not know Ubal as well as you think you do." He pauses. "You don't truly know Enya and Kundar, either."

My frustration is slowly turning into anger. "How can you say that? Enya and Kundar have been very good friends to me. And so has Ubal. I trust them all, especially Ubal."

Orion's gaze softens. "He is not the one for you, fair Ciran. Your heart belongs to another, someone who is worthy of you, only you have forgotten."

"What are you talking about?"

Orion closes his eyes, shaking his head. "Please, Ciran. I can say no more, but you will understand in time."

I have heard enough. "I must go," I say, retrieving my key from a small hook by the door. "I will meet Ubal downstairs."

I know the tone of dismissal in my voice is not missed by Orion, and I almost feel guilty for speaking to him so.

"Have you continued to read and study the scroll every day?" he suddenly asks. His voice has grown softer now, almost resigned, and his tone suggests that he already knows the answer.

Lowering my eyes, I swallow at the instant guilt rising inside me. I have not been as diligent as I should be with my reading. Somehow things always seem to come up that consume my time. Things I should not have put before my studying. After forgetting to read the scroll a couple of times, it became easier to forget. I have experienced feelings of guilt at times, as well as confusion, but it has became easier to push those feelings away as well. Being with Ubal makes it easier. Part of me wonders why this is. And going even deeper, another part of me knows it is wrong, but that part is always smothered when I am with Ubal. He makes everything all right. Besides, I still practice the teachings of the scroll. I will never go against them.

"I have studied enough that I will never forget what is written there," I finally say, looking into his eyes again. "I will be fine."

"Promise me you will begin again, Ciran," Orion pleads fervently. "Promise me you will study the scroll regularly, that you will never forsake it again."

Wanting to set his mind at ease, I smile, squeezing his hand. "I promise."

The sun is gifting its final rays of the day. Shops in the town square are beginning to close for the evening when a small, dark-haired bearded man jumps down from the carriage to greet his waiting passenger.

"Would you be heading to Fairmoor, sir?" he asks, opening the carriage door.

Isiral looks down at the man, his deep blue eyes showing surprise. "Why yes, but how . . .?"

"We were expecting you," the man answers merrily, his golden eyes twinkling beneath dark bushy brows.

Isiral picks up his bag and steps up into the carriage. Settling on the velvet cushioned seat, he pushes a strand of hair back from his face and heaves a deep sigh as he watches merchants putting away their wares for the evening. The nervousness he had felt previously is now, replaced by a sense of unexplainable urgency and anxiousness for the second part of his journey to begin. He places a strong hand on the velvety cushioned seat, lightly brushing his fingers back and forth against the soft material, his thoughts taking him in a million different directions.

His mind only holds a few memories from Krisandor, but he knows his purpose. He also knows there is something waiting for him. There are trials to be experienced, lessons to be learned, knowledge to be gained, and a battle to be fought. A battle in which the victory will bestow upon him something greater than life itself.

Blowing a light layer of dust away, the hunchback servant momentarily compares labels on the dark bottles. His master's cellar houses many brands of Splendorfire and he has a few favorites, but tonight his master had instructed him to bring a specific bottle. He squints, looking at the bottles a moment longer.

"Ah, jackpot!" he announces to himself.

Tonight is a special night for his master. He can feel it. The whole staff can, and the last thing he wants to do is upset his master. No, he does not want that. He has felt the wrath of his master's anger before. So have others. He has also been a recipient of many a reward at his master's hand. He prefers the latter without question.

Nothing is more important than pleasing his master. Nothing. For he owes his life, his very existence to his master.

For the servant, making his master happy is everything.

Yes, tonight everything has to be perfect.

The sun sets low in the gray mountainous peaks, and the magical backdrop reflects off the dark round cemented pool in the courtyard as I stroll around the grounds, my hand in the crook of Ubal's arm, his hand covering mine. I cast my eyes about, taking in my surroundings. Before arriving, I tried to picture his home, but I definitely had not pictured *this*.

We stop and I gaze over the water. Miniature stone lions stand around the base of the pool, their sculpted marble eyes glittering like gems. I take in the great granite fortress looming over the courtyard with its stained glass windows. Two larger stone lions stand on either side of the entrance, poised like sentinels standing guard. Dark moss grows around each head like a green mane.

"Your home is beautiful."

Ubal squeezes my hand. "Thank you. I hoped you would be pleased." Keeping my hand in his, he leads me across the large courtyard, past the tall lion statues to a set of metal double doors.

Just before we reach the doors, I glance up and see a bird, stranger than any I have ever seen before. It is perched on a thick flagpole extending from the side of the building. The creature is large and black with piercing red eyes, a blood red jagged beak, and enormous red and black striped claws. A stripe of green runs down its breast and one of its wings is bent upward at an odd angle, almost as if the bones are deformed.

The bird stars down at me, opening its jagged beak and exposing the inside of its dark mouth. The sight causes me to shudder inwardly. It is the only living thing I have seen around Ubal's home and I wondered at this fact. The surroundings are beautiful, yet cold in a way. I momentarily think of Kundar's estate. It is not as big as Ubal's, but the courtyard surrounding Kundar's light-gray granite home gives it a more inviting feel.

Still, except for the bird, Ubal's home is lovely. Pulling my eyes away from the strange creature, I smile at Ubal and he smiles back, and then holds one of the large doors open for me.

I shiver as we walk down the dimly lit corridor. He opens a set of wooden doors to the right and we enter the brightly-lit dining room. I marvel at its size and elegance. Crushed red velvet covers the walls and a long, dark wood table that looks large enough to accommodate twenty guests, is lined with dishes of food, the aroma of which makes my mouth water.

Forest green drapes, hanging in front of the large windows, are tied back with red tasseled ropes. There are two fireplaces, one on each end of the room. Both house roaring fires that permeate heat around the large room, giving it a feeling of coziness despite its ominous size. Above both fireplaces hang crests of some sort. They are painted black and red with gold lettering that I cannot read from where I stand. In the top left corner of each crest is a gold boar's head, to the right, some kind of horned animal. On the bottom left there is a crescent moon with three stars, and on the right, some kind of symbol that I cannot quite make out, paired with a scythe.

"I have been looking forward to having you come here," Ubal says, interrupting my observations. He guides me to one end of the table, pulling a chair out for me.

"I have been looking forward to being with you as well," I say, smiling at him. "Thank you for bringing me here."

"Oh, it is truly my pleasure."

When I am seated, Ubal sits at the head of the table. "Ah, Ciran," he says softly, "there is so much of myself I would like to share with you, so much of my world that you know nothing about. I want to share it all with you."

"I would like that as well." I am touched by his words.

He picks up a bottle of dark red liquid and pours two glasses. Smiling, he places one in front of me.

My eyes drop to the glass. In the past, each time Ubal has offered me Splendorfire, I have always declined, choosing to drink water instead. I have witnessed for myself the way it affects some people when consumed in excess. It strips away inhibitions and seems to take away all fear from a person. I remember Orion warning me to never be tempted by the drink, that it is one of the many things on the journey that changes people, deterring them from the path, causing them to become lost.

But how can the absence of fear be bad?

My friends do not seem lost to me. They seem very happy and content, especially Ubal. Maybe it only affects some people in adverse ways. Maybe some people are experienced enough to handle it better than others. Besides, I don't think Ubal would ask me to try it if it is really so terrible. He cares about me.

I ponder on how Ubal has never pushed me to try the drink and has always accepted my answer when I refuse. He has been so understanding, I begin to wonder if there would be any harm in trying a little. Most of the people I know indulge in the drink, and for the most part, they seem okay. Surely it wouldn't hurt to try a little.

On the indulgence of Splendorfire rest all other weakness that are sure to follow. Orion's words are shrouded in the confusion of all my other thoughts.

Ubal smiles, tapping the glass. "There are many brands, but this is one of my favorites. I would love it if you would try a bit." He grins. "I promise you will like it. And if you do not, I shall make it up to you."

I laugh softly. Then, mentally coming to a decision, I pick up the goblet, and before I can change my mind I quickly raise it to my lips.

Ubal sits back and smiles, his dark gray eyes instantly brightening.

I sip the burgundy liquid, smiling as I lower the glass. "It tastes wonderful," I say with a light laugh. I take another sip, and then place the glass on the table before sitting back.

There. No flash of lightening, I muse. *The world is not*

suddenly coming to an end. I only took a couple of little sips and I am fine. Feeling satisfied that I have done nothing wrong, I turned my attention to the various dishes of food. "Everything looks delicious."

There are platters of sliced pork, beef, roasted chicken, mini skewers of vegetables, a bowl of potatoes dripping with butter and seasoned with garlic and parsley, and five different kinds of bread. The desserts consist of a variety of fruit tarts, miniature frosted cakes, creamy custard, and a tray of fresh fruit. It is enough food to feed a room full of people.

"My cook is very good and I have become somewhat spoiled, I'm afraid. He can whip up whatever I wish, so there is always variety on the menu." He gestures to the food. "Shall we start?"

I nod, anxious to try a little of everything. The food at Havenwood is always delicious, but I am excited about trying some new dishes. Maybe I will even pass some suggestions on to the cook at Havenwood. The customers would probably enjoy some new dishes as well.

Leaning forward, I reach for the tray of sliced beef, swaying a bit as a strange warmth begins to spread through me. With this warmth comes a feeling unlike anything I have ever experienced. I feel relaxed, yet uptight, too. Attempting to steady myself and quell the strange sensation, I smile, absently scratching my wrist.

Ubal quietly studies me for a moment, then reaches for my hand. "I am so pleased you are here, Ciran." He wraps his cool fingers loosely around my wrist. "I am so pleased," he repeats.

The gentle pressure of his fingers seems to calm the itch and my eyes are drawn to his hypnotic gaze. After a moment, I am startled as I watch the color of his eyes change from gray to brown, finally settling to a coal black.

Almost immediately, the warm sensation spreading through me begins to change and a sudden coldness seeps into my body, instantly chilling me until I shiver. I attempt to pull my arm away, but the pressure of Ubal's hand increases.

Pressing my free hand against my forehead, I try to clear away the haziness in my head and swallow back the rising nausea. At this moment my only thought is getting back to my room at Havenwood.

"I feel ill, Ubal," I manage to say, my speech slurred. "I need to leave."

Ubal moves closer. "It is all right, my Ciran. Do not fight it. Give in to it."

My mind is so cloudy, Ubal's words sound jumbled.

What is happening to me? I try to clear my thoughts, continually swallowing against the nausea.

"Please, Ubal," I plead, squeezing my eyes shut, pulling my wrist free.

Ubal sighs, standing. "There is no need to return to Havenwood," he says, smiling down at me, only the voice that was once so smooth is now harsh and gravelly. I finally open my eyes and look up at him, and what I see makes my blood run even colder despite my impaired mind.

The scaly patch normally showing beneath the opening of Ubal's robe has grown and expanded, and now covers his entire face. I watch in horror as his hands change, becoming dark gray, his once fair skin seeming to peel away before my very eyes. The hair that had been a glorious brown is now a murky gray, coarse and thin, and balding on the top. He is repulsive!

Struggling to stand, I weakly push myself up from the chair and begin to back away, holding on to the edge of the table to steady myself, trying to keep from falling. This is a nightmare, one that I cannot seem to wake up from no matter how desperately I try.

"What are you?" I whisper, my eyes wide.

"I am but a man, Ciran. A man who possesses power beyond your comprehension. A man who can grant you your every wish if you will but give in to me. Give in to my power. You are already mine. All you need do is accept it.

Accept your fate."

No! I frantically shake my head as he continues to move closer. "Stay away from me!" I cry, lifting a hand to shield myself. As I raise arms, my hazy vision is immediately drawn to my wrist and I am even more shocked by what I see.

"No!" I whisper as my eyes take in the light gray patch of skin that had only itched earlier. I slowly raise my eyes to his again as realization dawns on me. My internal question about the 'skin ailment' is now answered with an absolute clarity that instantly brings a crushing sorrow to my heart and soul.

"Yes," Ubal affirms softly, reading the dawning of truth in my eyes. "There is no use fighting it anymore, Ciran. You are mine now. I have branded you, just as I have branded everyone else." He slowly moves closer, like a vulture closing in on its prey, his black eyes glowing red.

"The deed has been done. I have found a weakness in you. Now you are exactly where I want you."

"No!" I cry, backing away.

"Yes, my dear. You know as well as I that you belong with me. No one can resist me. Ask Enya and Kundar. They will tell you this is the right path for you. It is a popular and well worn one."

"No, no, no!" I continue to cry, my voice growing weaker. My back is pressed against the cold wall. I am trapped, and I am terrified, not only of Ubal, but of the choice I have made tonight, the choice that now finds me in such a cold place, not only physically but emotionally as well. Why did I not listen to Orion? He told me I didn't know Ubal or Enya and Kundar as well as I thought. He tried to warn me, but I refused to listen, as if I possessed more knowledge than he did. Now I am suffering the dark, disdainful consequences of my arrogant and thoughtless actions.

Staring at the hideous creature, my skin begins to crawl even more. Ubal is so close, I can feel the dampness of his stale breath on her face, smell the rank odor of his scaly skin.

"Please don't," I plead once more.

"I promise you, Ciran, if you will just give in and let go, all will be well and your journey will be a breeze. I will make it easy for you. I have the power to make it so."

I desperately try to close my mind, for his words are beginning to weaken me. I can feel my strength waning.

I have been such a fool. Such a fool. And now I am left all alone to this end . . . and it is all my fault.

"No," I whisper a final time as Ubal reaches out to touch my face. I turn my head away. My soul is almost drained of strength. I slide down the wall, my back scraping against the rough stone beneath the velvet, my body completely weakened.

A victorious smile spreads across Ubal's face. She will be his. Finally, she will belong to him. Oh, how he has looked forward to this day! How he has spent years preparing for it! She is in no shape to leave or even move for that matter. Before this night is over–before the next moment had passed–she will submit to him. He will see it done and revel in the victory.

Before Ubal's hand can make contact with Ciran's skin, a burst of light enters the room. Ubal turns, his dark skin paling slightly and his eyes burning as they fall upon the source.

In the midst of the brilliant light stands Orion. His fiery red hair is now transformed to a lustrous golden mane, billowing around his powerfully majestic frame. His skin glows and his golden eyes are bright and piercing. His enlarged muscular form is clothed in a shimmering white robe, a golden sword strapped to his waist. He stands tall, his height now seven feet, and his massive hands form fists as his eyes level on Ubal.

Coming to, I slowly open my eyes, attempting to adjust my gaze. After a moment I recognize Orion. Taking in his glorious form, I know I must be on the edge of death. Never have I seen anything so beautiful. Even in my weakened state, I can feel his power, and the warmth he radiates. Soaking in this warmth, my eyes slowly close and I give in to the beckoning darkness, too spent to fight it any longer.

Ubal grins, exposing yellow jagged teeth. He crouches down with his back to Ciran, like an animal protecting its prey. Black saliva drips from his mouth, running down his chin, the thick droplets foaming like acid as they land on the stone floor. "You are too late, Guardian! She is mine now! She strayed from the teachings of the scroll. She has tasted of the forbidden drink, therefore she is lost to you!"

"Nay, Collector of the Lost!" comes Orion's powerful voice, shaking the room like thunder, causing several stones in the ceiling to crumble. "She is far from lost, and well you know it!" He moves forward, each step leaving a shimmering footprint on the dark floor. "You may lay claim, but this one is strong. I feel it. Her strength is what brought me here. You shall not have her."

"She is already mine!" Ubal snarls, jutting his hideous face forward.

Orion swiftly draws the golden sword from its scabbard.

Ubal quickly backs away, his eyes seething with hatred because of the power of light Orion possesses. He watches, completely powerless as the brilliant being lifts the young woman in his arms.

Orion turns to Ubal, his fiery gaze fixed. "You may claim many a weak soul, Collector of the Lost, but never the strong chosen few."

Then, in a flash of light, he is gone.

Orion

Holding the unconscious young woman against him and riding the white mare at full speed, Orion opens his thoughts to telepathic communication.

I have her now. She is weak, but she will be all right.

There is a relieved sigh followed by a response. *Thank you, my friend. However, this is far from over. You must prepare her for that.*

Do not worry, Orion assures. *All will be well.*

"Hold on, fair Ciran," he whispers into the wind as they ride in haste, the thunderous sound of the horse's hooves beating like a drum against the hard terrain. "Hold on."

Grinding his jagged teeth, Ubal sits down at the food-laden table. He picks up the goblet Ciran had sipped from and raises it to his own twisted and deformed lips.

One evening. All he had needed was one full evening and she would have been his. He would have possessed her, owned her. She had been on her way to an eternal life in his world and it would have crushed his enemy, her father, Cillian.

He almost had her. It had been slow, but he had found an opening. Granted, compared to most, her foolish choice had been small, but it was there. It was to be the beginning of her downfall. He had been patient, and his patience had begun to pay off. He just hadn't been quick enough.

Well, he muses with a smile, *no matter. She has been branded. It is only a matter of time. Soon I will prove once and for all that weakness runs in the family.*

Isiral

Isiral wipes the beads of perspiration from his forehead. Laying back on the damp sheet, he brushes the tangle of hair from his face and stares up into the darkness, trying to slow the mad pounding of his heart. The nightmare had been brutal, for in it, he saw the enemy he has yet to meet. He couldn't see the victim's face, but he could see Ubal through his or her eyes. He saw the hideously scaly face, the jagged teeth, the red eyes. He smelled the foulness of his breath and felt the coldness of his hands. He could feel the pain and anguish of the victim. He could feel the cold evil that had surrounded the forlorn being. The person was hurting fiercely, suffering beyond words.

Then when it seemed that the victim had no strength left, there had suddenly come a blinding light, and with it came a warmth that was indescribable. It had immediately begun to soothe the anguish and chase the darkness away. Somehow through the dream, Isiral felt everything the person felt. He doesn't know how or why, but he did. One thing is certain. He knows the enemy now. He will see through the facade he is sure Ubal will have in place. He feels deep sorrow for the person suffering now at Ubal's hand.

Feeling the pain anew, Isiral heaves a deep sigh, then turning to his side, he presses his face into the pillow and sobs.

Seven

Chosen Path

A light dew dots the outside of my window as morning dawns clear and bright. Chirping birds fly merrily to and fro, oblivious to the newly-hurting soul residing in the building they stop and perch upon.

I take in the picture through swollen puffy eyes. My pillow is wet and stained from the tears I cried through the night. Now as coherent thoughts fully awakens in my mind, the tears begin again. I try to find comfort in the gentle hand caressing my hair, but my heart is inconsolable.

I failed. I had been weak and disobedient, and I failed. I let myself be deceived, allowed myself to be seduced by disguised and cunning evil. And for what? A moment of misguided pleasure. It was all a lie. The happiness I felt had been an illusion, and I fell for it, had given into weakness.

I failed.

"Oh, Orion," I whisper through the tears, my hoarse voice cutting through the silence of my room. "Why did you not tell me?" I release a small sob. "Why did you not tell me?"

"I could not," comes Orion's gentle response. He brushes the hair back from my face. "I can only give you guidance, not tell you what will be."

I rest my eyes on his face. His appearance has returned to normal. Thinking back on how he looked when he came to my rescue causes a shudder of sorrowful amazement to come over me. My eyes fill once again.

"I am so sorry," I sob. "I am so sorry I did not listen. You tried to warn me, but . . . I am so sorry."

"Shhh," he soothes, continuing to caress my hair. "All is not lost, fair Ciran."

At the sound of the last two words, I sit up, angrily shoving my arm out, exposing the dark patch of skin on my wrist. "I am not fair! Look at this. This happened because I did not listen, because I was weak. I did this, and it cannot be undone. So you see, I *am* lost." My lips begin to tremble, my pain renewed.

Orion takes my wrist in his hand and gently runs his fingers across the scaly area before looking into my swollen eyes.

"All is not lost," he repeats. "The reason I was able to come to your aid is because you resisted Ubal's evil. Most do not. I have found that when a person chooses to taste the forbidden drink, unless he or she fights against Ubal's power, the brand has usually spread by morning. Yours has not. Once others have had a taste of Splendorfire, inhibitions are no more and they have no desire to turn back. Take Enya and Kundar for example. It is not just the indulgence of Splendorfire that brands them. That was only the beginning, the catalyst of what was to come. No, Ciran, for them it is indulging in acts that should only be approached after a man and woman have been bound by marriage.

"Then there are Rena, Cara, and Lalan, the three women who work the morning shift in the kitchen. Their brand spreads because of dishonesty and deceit. And poor Fallon will forever regret giving into the weakness of the forbidden drink, because from that weakness sprung many others. She is one of the very few who actually feels grief over her choices." He sighs. "These are only a few of the many evils brought on by the forbidden drink created by the dark lords centuries ago."

"But Ubal told me there was no turning back now."

"Ubal is a master of lies. Yes, you have made a grave choice, but you are also very strong. Hold onto that strength. If you do, your way is sure. This brand will not always be so, fair Ciran."

Releasing my wrist, he stands and walks over to the dresser. Placing his hand on the drawer handle, he looks back at me, as if to ask for permission. When I nod, he opens the drawer and lifts the crystal pendant from its resting place. He brings the pendant to me, placing it in my hand.

"Choice is an individual thing and each of us is responsible for our own." He pauses, looking at the crystal in my hand. It catches the sunlight coming through the window, its brilliance as bright as a beacon shining through the darkest night. "There are two paths before you, and there are people eager to lead you on both paths." He looks into my eyes intently. "Which one will you choose?"

Smiling, he wipes my tears, then stands and presses a kiss to my forehead. "Choose, Ciran. Just choose."

Saying nothing more, he turns and leaves.

I stare at the door long after he is gone, pondering deeply his final admonition. Can it really be that simple? How can this choice undo the previous one that is now etched into my skin? How can I ever make up for such weakness?

Regardless of how, I know I have to try. Otherwise, the misery surrounding me will completely take over and will surely be my undoing.

Choice.

It all comes down to choice. It *is that* simple.

Mentally making a decision, I dry my tears. Then, taking a deep breath, I unscrew the crystal.

I am grateful I don't have to work today. It allows me to spend the entire morning in study and meditation. I don't even stop to eat. I have no appetite for food. My hunger goes much deeper. It is a hunger of the spirit. I thirst for the knowledge and guidance that can only be quenched by the principles taught in the scroll. And each moment I spend in study brings a refreshment to me that can't be rivaled by even the coolest drink of water on the hottest of days. The sensation is glorious and I wonder how I could have abandoned something that brings me so much joy. How had I not missed the peace that comes from my studies?

Now, as I think back on the time I spent with Ubal, I realize I hadn't truly been happy. I couldn't possibly have been content when the very core of what is right and good had been missing. I thought I was holding to the scroll's teachings during that time, and nothing could pull me away, but I was mistaken. I was blinded by Ubal's subtle ability to make evil seem good and good seem evil. I can see it all so clearly now, even as I sit reading over a particular principle of the scroll.

> ***Seek after knowledge to gain true understanding, for only then can wisdom be obtained.***

Remembering the conversation I had with Ubal on that very subject, I can see how easily he twisted that principle. Two questions repeatedly run through my mind. How could I have let it happen, and what will I do to keep it from happening again?

Reaching deep into my soul, I unearth the answer to both questions.

Wandering aimlessly as I ponder everything that has happened, I find myself back in the silent, dimly-lit corridor. My steps are measured and sure as I approach the familiar statue of the man bearing grapes. The secret smile is very familiar, as is his face. For the face is Ubal's.

I know you now. I know that smile. I also know the true

face behind the facade. I mistakenly trusted you, blindly followed you like a lost lamb, separated from her flock and in need of milk from her mother, only to find that I was being led into a wolves' den. I could not see the beast lurking behind the beauty.

Taking a deep breath, I move closer until my face is an inch away from that of the statue's.

"I assure you," I whisper, "that will never happen again."

Tonight I dream.

I am running through a maze of overgrown jasmine and wisteria bushes. The sky is dark and thunder roars as rain begins to come down in sheets. I run blindly, unable to see two feet in front of me, and no matter which way I turn, I run into a thick wall of bushes. Branches reach out and tear at my soaked robe, pulling at my drenched hair.

Hot tears spill down my cheeks and mingle with the rain as I frantically search for a way out, but the harder I try, the more the walls seem to close in on me.

I am trapped, like a bird in a cage.

"Give up, Ciran," comes a mocking voice. "This is pointless. You will never find your way out."

I immediately recognize the voice. I could pick Ubal's gravelly voice out of a thousand voices. Closing my mind to the sound of it, I continue to frantically search for a way out.

"You will fail because you are weak!" The voice grows louder. "You will never make it!"

I finally reach a turn that looks different from the rest.

"Yes, Ciran," comes a new voice–a gentle voice. "Yes, my angel, you have found the way."

With new incentive now, I forge ahead, instinctively taking the correct turns and curves without thought.

Suddenly there is sunlight and warmth. I lift my arms, savoring the feel of it against my skin. I have made it. I escaped the clutches of the dark. I am free.

Awakening, I stare up into the darkness, touching the scaly patch on my arm.

A dream. It was only a dream.

"Not quite free yet," I whisper into the silence, wiping a tear away. "Maybe one day."

Through the weeks, I continue to study the scroll with a voraciousness that is beyond description, internalizing its teachings until they become a part of me. The change inside me is steady as I face each new day unwavering in my journey.

Sadly, the friendship I once treasured with Enya and Kundar is no more. They have abandoned me because my chosen path is different from theirs. Though I am pained by this loss, it is nothing compared to the pain my previous choice cost me. I am reminded of that pain daily each time my gaze falls to my wrist.

Still, the loss of one friendship has strengthened another. I have a bond with Orion, one that has grown stronger with the passing of time. He is always there for me and I know he ever will be. He is my guardian, my teacher, my confidant. I could not ask for a better friend, and I need a friend more now than ever. Orion is stability, the one constancy in my changing world. Without his guidance I know I truly would be lost.

As time goes by I notice I am no longer greeted as 'fair Ciran' by anyone except Orion. I miss that title more than I thought I would. One unguarded moment changed everything, including the way others look at me. The regular customers are still cordial, but I feel the difference in them and it hurts. It is almost as if the patrons are sorrowful, as if I let them down somehow. They are all branded as well, but I am being treated differently. Maybe I had been an unspoken hope for them, a hope that said it is possible to exist in this world spared from scarring and untouched by weakness. Now I have taken that hope away. If only I knew how to give it back.

My coworkers are civil, but the comfortable rapport we once shared is no longer there. It is now replaced by occasional aloofness on their part, and I understand why. If I had chosen to travel along the same path they are, everything would be fine, but instead I chose to go against the grain, and that just isn't done. They are so different from the customers I serve. One group of people seems a little sorrowful, while the other seems content. I occasionally ponder this fact.

Working with Enya is the hardest because I can no longer chat and share secret thoughts and dreams with her as I once could. I have tried a few times to salvage our friendship by inviting Enya to share meals with me, asking her to see a couple of plays, and even inviting her to go for walks. Enya never accepts my invitations and is very cold in her refusals.

I have even tried to start up casual conversations with Enya, but I am always given the cold shoulder. I receive the same treatment from Kundar. Whenever he comes to pick Enya up for the evening, if I am near, he completely ignores me, like I am invisible to his eyes. I finally give up and accept that our friendship is truly finished. I never guessed how my choice to live by the scroll would change others. Still, I am determined to do the best I can and not become discouraged.

Part Three
Healing

Eight

Sakriel

"I shall always be with you. You will carry me with you."

My eyes open as the familiar gentle voice fills my mind. It is the third time this week that the voice has resonated inside my head like an echo of some distant memory. The sound of it always fills me with a deep sense of longing, yet it also brings me such comfort, I want to cry. The two emotions are conflicting, but they are here, coexisting inside me, and they are real–more real than anything I have ever felt before.

Sometimes another distant memory follows the voice. It

111

is the memory of a man standing inside a gate, gazing at me. A breeze lifts his golden hair. His face is never clear no matter how hard I concentrate on the vision, but I know it is me his eyes are fixed upon. Each time the memory fades, I experience an unexplainable heartache.

"Why can I not remember?" I whisper, a deep sigh escaping me. The question is always met with silence.

Deciding that some fresh air will do me good, I get up from my chair next to the window and walk over and kneel by a wooden chest at the foot of the bed. Opening it, I pull out a light blanket and drape it over my arm. I then take the door key from a hook on the wall and leave my room.

Sitting in the field behind Havenwood among the tall grass and wildflowers, I gaze out at the backdrop of shimmering gray mountains. The picture vividly brings to mind another beautiful mountainous view that is similar to this one, only more glorious. After a brief moment the picture fades, leaving me once again longing for a place I can't remember. Closing my eyes, I try to recapture the vision, and for an instant I succeed, but before I can even draw a breath, it is gone again.

Opening my eyes, I watch a couple of butterflies hovering over a yellow wildflower. They flutter back and forth, one chasing the other as if they are involved in some sort of mating game. I study them as they momentarily landed on the flower, fascinated by the gracefulness of their gently fluttering wings, and marvel at their beauty.

Oh, if I could only be as carefree as one of these marvelous creatures, if only for a day.

When the butterflies finally fly away, I keep my gaze fixed on the flower. Feeling relaxed, a feeling of drowsiness slowly descends upon me. Closing my heavy eyelids, a familiar peaceful scene appears.

I am walking among a forest of tall trees with a beautiful golden-winged being. The scent of pine is thick in the air and we are surrounded by the friendly company of deer, rabbits, squirrels, and chipmunks. We laugh as we hold hands and share our secret dreams with one another through thought.

We smile as a smaller winged being appears before us. Then we lift her and spin her around, relishing the sound of her laughter.

"Mother, Aunt Ciran," the child mentally relays, "come and see the treasure I have found."

"All right," the mother relays to her daughter.

As the two walk away, the woman turns to me and says,

"Wait. Look, he comes."

Instantly, the drowsiness falls away and I open my eyes. Turning, I see a lone figure moving in the distance. I watch unblinking as the person draws nearer, his gait telling me he must be someone of great importance, for he walks like royalty. His broad shoulders are straight and his step is sure, his eyes ever fixed on me. When he finally reaches me, my lips part and I stare up at him in awe.

It is as if I am looking at my own reflection, only his features are clearly more masculine. His shoulder-length, dark hair and golden skin shimmer in the sun, and his emerald eyes sparkle as he smiles down at me. His white robe is trimmed in silver and glitters in the bright light of day, and the muscles of his tall frame are well defined. He is completely magnificent, without flaw or blemish. He is walking perfection.

"I know you," I whisper, my heart leaping as I continue to stare at the man.

He kneels in front of me, taking my hand in his. "Yes, you do, fair Ciran."

Though his voice is like music, the resonance of it warming me, his statement causes my smile to fade, for his words concerning me are untrue.

"I am not fair," I say, looking away.

He reaches out and covers my branded wrist with his hand, pressing the other against my cheek, turning my face back to his. "Why do you say that?" he asks gently.

Touched by his compassion, tears quickly fill my eyes. "Because I made a choice that I can never take back. I will bear the scar of that choice forever, and everyone who sees me will know how weak I am."

His hand tightens on my wrist slightly. "You are strong, stronger than you realize, and one day soon you will come to know that."

I manage to smile through the tears. "Who are you to me?" I ask, taking in his handsome features.

He looks at me thoughtfully for a moment. "Would you believe me if I said I was your brother?"

I lower my gaze to the large hand still covering the branded area of my wrist. His skin tone matches my own perfectly. "I would," I softly answer, lifting my eyes to his again. I stare at him intently for a moment. "You came here for me, did you not?"

He nods.

"What is your name?"

"Sakriel, little one."

At his answer, a distant memory of him is suddenly before me. It seems to come from nowhere and its intensity is greater than any past vision I have been gifted with. I place my hand over the one covering my wrist. "You have called me that before," I say in awe.

"I have, many times." He quietly studies me for a moment. "Do you trust me, little one?"

"Yes," I answer without hesitation.

Sakriel sighs. "Then trust me when I tell you that you are fair." With that, he slowly lifts his hand from my wrist.

I look down and gasp, blinking several times to make sure I am really seeing what I think I see. The brand is no longer there. My wrist is now as smooth and clear as the rest of my arm. I turn it over and back again, amazed that the mark is really gone. Tears profusely stream down my face. "How?" is all I can voice, emotion thick in my throat.

Sakriel smiles. "It is a gift given to me at the finish of my journey. But how is not as important as why, and there are two answers to that question. The first is because you desperately wanted to be free of the brand. The second is because you trusted me." He gently presses a hand to my cheek. "You are my sister, Ciran, my flesh and blood, and I am here for you."

Unable to help it, I lean forward, throwing my arms around his neck. "Thank you."

"You are welcome," he whispers against my hair.

"You will stay?" I murmur against his shoulder, wondering if this is the only reason he has come. "I have felt so lost and alone. Please stay."

He draws back a little, a grin lighting his beautiful face. "What of Orion? I dare say he would be offended if he knew his presence meant so little." His voice is teasing.

"I adore Orion," I answer with a trembling smile, my voice penitent. "I will always be grateful for his presence and his guidance, but you are my brother. Please stay."

Sakriel pulls me close, pressing a kiss into her hair. "I promise, little one, I will always be here."

I ease back a little and wipe my face before taking Sakriel's hands in mine. "Tell me about our father. I can't remember anything about him, but I know he must be loving and kind, because I hear his voice often."

Sakriel folds his legs and moves closer and I do the same, our knees touching, our hands still clasped. "He *is* loving and kind, and we look like him."

"Does he think of me?"

"Every day. Every moment. His heart ached when you had to leave. Your absence has been hard on him. He misses you much, much more than words can express."

I give him a sad smile. "I miss him as well. How can that be when I do not remember him?"

Plucking a wildflower and twirling it between his fingers, he says, "Part of you did not forget him. In time you will remember him fully." He smiles. "You, me, and Father used to sit for hours and talk. It did not matter what we discussed, we just treasured being together. We had picnics together in the courtyard, went to dinner parties of friends, and sometimes you and I would play games with the young children in the kingdom. And you were a voracious reader."

"I still am."

"I thought so," he says with a twinkle in his eye.

Remembering the experience I had just before my brother appeared, I say, "Sakriel, before you came, I had a dream, or at least I think it was a dream. I was walking through the woods with a beautiful woman with golden skin and hair, and she had wings. We talked to one another, yet our lips did not move."

Sakriel smiles, squeezing my hand. "You were remembering Mazina. She is an Inchant, and your best friend."

With his words, memories of the Inchant woman and her people instantly flood my mind. I remember often visiting Mazina's home in the forest. I remember how strong and graceful the Inchant people are. And with the memories comes a longing to see my friend again.

"Is she well," I ask, wishing I could talk with Mazina.

"Yes," Sakriel answers. "And she misses you."

"I miss her as well." I chuckle as the memories continue. "Oh, what fun we used to have playing with her children!"

Sakriel laughs, too. "They were a rambunctious brood, were they not?"

"They were," I agree, laughing softly.

After a moment, I cast a sobering gaze across the tall grass, my thoughts suddenly traveling in a million different directions. I turn back to my brother, hesitant to ask the question poised on the tip of my tongue, but I know I must.

"Sakriel, tell me about Ubal."

My brother's expression changes, his emerald eyes darkening. Closing them, he takes a deep breath before he speaks. "Ciran, Ubal is the vilest of creatures. He is the most powerful dark lord who has ever lived. He gained his power by disposing of all the other dark lords. Now he is the only one. His mission is to turn as many souls as he can into lost ones so he can own them and have power over them, enabling him to control them. This is why he is called Collector of the Lost. He will stop at nothing to keep as many people as possible from completing their journey in this world. Once he lays hold on a person they usually submit to his will."

Sudden chills sweep through me despite the heat of the day. As I think about Enya, Kundar, and many others I know who have been seduced by Ubal's power, a sense of sadness quickly comes over me. "Why do they not break free? Surely they can."

"Yes," Sakriel says gently, "but they must choose to do it. He cannot hold a person unless they willingly submit to him. Sadly, they are seduced by his declaration of making one's journey easy. Once a person chooses to believe his lies, unless he or she has a change of heart and a strong desire to break free, that person is lost, and Ubal has won another soul."

He squeezes my hand. "You were strong enough to resist, little one, and because of that, Orion was able to assist you, but it is not over." He pauses, his eyes darkening even more. "Your resistance has only made him more determined to keep you from finishing your journey."

I shiver again. "Was it the same for you when you were here?"

"It was," he answers solemnly.

"Yet you did not weaken as I did." Shame enters me once again as I say this.

He presses a gentle hand to my cheek. "It is a hard road, Ciran, and you are by far stronger than most. Father is very proud of you."

" But . . . how did you do it, Sakriel? How did you exist here without weakening?"

"I knew that I must," he answers simply.

"But *how* did you do it?" I repeat as a tear rolls down my cheek. It still hurts to think of how weak I had been.

Sakriel catches one of my tears with his finger. Looking into my eyes, he repeats, "I knew that I must. And now you do as well."

I swallow hard against a fresh rise of emotion. "I do not have your strength."

"Yes, you do," he says, lifting my chin with his finger. "You do because you know now that you are not alone in this."

Looking down at our joined hands, I whisper, "I hope I will not fail."

Sakriel

Sakriel's smile is sad as he studies his sister's down-turned head. He loves her greatly, yet he knows what tests are ahead of her and what part they will both play in the future of this world, as well as that of Krisandor. He knows the real reason things will be so different for *her*.

"You will not fail, little one," he whispers, pulling her to him. "You have the power of the *most* powerful behind you and *in* you. You will not fail."

Nine

Friends

Sitting in the carriage across from my brother, I smile as we travel to the town square. I have only been back once since arriving in Havenwood, and I have been looking forward to shopping and seeing the sights of the town. Since I have always kept close to home, my wages have accumulated substantially and I am anxious to purchase a much needed new wardrobe. I also want to purchase something special for Sakriel and Orion. The two men mean more to me than I can possibly express in words. They are my best friends, and deep inside I know I would never be able to continue on my journey without having them to lean on. I am truly grateful for their presence in my life.

Orion brings the carriage to a stop in front of a long row of shops. He immediately jumps down and opens the door for us. I smile warmly as he takes my hand and helps me down.

Glancing down the street in either direction, there are a few people moving about, purchasing diverse pieces of merchandise. The people in town seem happy to me, and free of contention. People smile and laugh, and the whole area is clean and has a peaceful feel to it. It is rather calming.

I glance at Orion and he smiles up at me, seeming to read my thoughts. "There is no crime here because of the presence of the gateway back to the Place of Learning." He directs my gaze to the spot where he had first picked me up. "The entrance is not visible, but it is there, and only those who finish their journey are allowed to see the gate again and enter. Once a person is admitted back, he prepares to reenter Krisandor and return to his home and those he left behind. Those who have made a conscious choice not to finish their journey and are content in their corruption stay far away from this part of town. Ubal has corrupted so many that very few people come here now. Business has declined for the shopkeepers, but somehow they manage to stay open." He pauses, his gaze moving around the square. "There is peace here."

A comforting warmth comes over me as I listen to Orion.

How I long to go back through that gate. The brief glimpses of the life I once lived continually beckons me, and the desire to reclaim that life grows stronger with each passing day.

There is still one thing, however, that puzzles me. It is something I have thought and wondered about since remembering the paintings in the Place of Learning the week before. I can't believe I had not thought of it sooner–like after I arrived at Havenwood.

"Orion, why are there no children? I haven't seen any the entire time I have been here. There were paintings of children on the wall in the Place of Learning, so I know they are in Krisandor. But why not here?"

Orion smiles. "I knew the question would come to you one day. Evil touches the people here in many ways. There are no children because a child cannot live inside a woman who has been branded. The moment branding occurs, unless it is reversed, those life giving elements are destroyed. That is why the earth is becoming so restless. The evil has grown so much, even the land feels it."

I visibly shudder at his words. He places a comforting hand on my arm and I draw forth a smile, thinking of how grateful I am that my brand is no more. I don't know if I will ever have the opportunity to become a mother, but it is wonderful to know I would be able to give a child life.

Moving my eyes back to the shops, I notice that the entrance of each tent has a brightly-colored rug placed before it. The various shades of red, pink, yellow, green, and orange stand out and catch the eye of visitors in the square.

While Orion visits with the merchant of a produce stand and Sakriel examines some jewelry in another small shop, I enter a nearby shop selling robes and gowns for every occasion. I am promptly greeted by a beautiful woman wearing an incredible red gown trimmed in silver and gold-twined rope. With her graying black hair, flawless skin, and gray eyes, she is absolutely stunning.

The woman smiles. "Hello. My name is Halia."

"I am Ciran."

"What can I help with today, miss?"

"Well, I would like to purchase some robes and a gown."

"We have some beautiful colors, all of which would look stunning on you, I'm sure."

"Thank you," I say, feeling my cheeks color slightly.

Halia picks out several robes and gowns for me to try on. Each one draws a wide smile from the woman when she sees them on me. "You look beautiful, fair Ciran, no matter what color you wear."

Fair Ciran. My smile is wide, happiness and gratitude filling me that I am now being addressed as 'fair Ciran' again.

"Thank you," I say, mentally vowing to never again do anything that would make me unworthy of that title.

"May I ask you something?" Halia asks as she folds the garments I have chosen.

"Certainly."

"Are you new here?"

"No, I live at Havenwood, but I don't get into town much."

"Ah," Halia says with a smile. "That is why I have never seen you. Well, are you enjoying your outing today?"

"I am very much."

"Are you here alone?"

"No, I am with my brother and a friend."

"Well, since you have finished picking out your things, would you have some time to visit for a bit? Business has been rather slow lately and I don't get to do that much anymore."

I nod, grateful she asked. "I would love to. I know very few people outside of Havenwood."

"Well, then after we take care of our transaction, have a seat and I will get us each a drink of cool water. It is pretty warm out today and a drink sounds refreshing."

"That it does," I agree. I take some money from my pocket and pay her for the robes and gown. Halia wraps them and hands the package to me before leaving the room.

Walking across the tent, I sit down on an intricately carved wooden bench. I run my fingers over the floral carvings for a moment, admiring the beautiful handiwork before placing my package on the bench beside me. I glance around the spacious room. There are numerous robes and gowns hanging from poles lining the walls of the tent. There is a table with hair combs, accented in various stones. Crystal, amethyst, turquoise, pearl, ruby, sapphire, and emerald jewels are beautifully set upon the silver and gold combs. The black velvet cloth beneath makes the jewels sparkle with brilliance.

There are also hand painted masks with glittering jewels and colorful feathers hanging from metal stands placed here and there. I cannot get over all the lovely things and decide that before I leave, I will purchase a couple of the combs.

"Here we are." Halia reenters the room with two goblets of cold water and hands one to me.

"Thank you very much," I say, taking a sip.

"You are welcome, and thank you for agreeing to visit with me." She sits on a stool across from me. "I have had the privilege of staying at Havenwood before. It is a very lovely place."

"It is," I agree. "I have been very happy there."

Halia nods, sipping her water. "I remember the food there being wonderful."

"Aga is a very good cook. I am told she has been there for many years and is actually the best cook to ever hold the position there."

"Well, I shall have to come and dine there again sometime. Perhaps I can even persuade you to join me."

"I work the day shift, but if you should decide to stop in for an evening meal I would be happy to dine with you."

"Wonderful," she says, her smile wide. "I will make it a point to come this week. Then maybe we can get to know each other better."

"I would like that."

"Having no family gets pretty lonely. Sometimes I find myself conversing with air." She chuckles. "You should see the looks I get from people sometimes. They probably think I'm a crazy old woman."

"Oh, I doubt that," I say, grinning. "And you look far from old. Although I am told we are all older than we know."

Halia's brow lifts slightly. "How true. Indeed, we are all older than we seem."

I am just finishing my water when Sakriel enters. I stand and introduce the two.

"Sakriel, this is Halia. She owns the shop."

"Hello," Sakriel says, his smile slightly guarded.

"I am pleased to meet you," Halia says. "It has been wonderful getting acquainted with your sister. I hope we can become friends."

"I hope so as well," I tell her. Since I have no friends now besides Orion and my brother, the prospect of making a new one is exciting.

"Are you ready?" Sakriel asks, picking up my package.

"Yes, I believe I am. Oh, wait, I almost forgot." I turn back to Halia. "I wanted to purchase some of your beautiful combs."

"All right," she says, moving over to the table. "Which ones would you like?"

I pick out two emerald combs, smiling when Sakriel says they match my eyes. I joke that they would look lovely on him too since we share the same eye coloring.

"It has been a pleasure," I say to Halia after paying. "I hope to see you soon."

"You will, fair Ciran." She smiles. "That is a promise."

Nodding to her, Sakriel takes my hand in his and escorts me from the shop.

"She was very nice," I say to Sakriel as we walk across the street to another shop. I thoroughly enjoyed my visit with Halia and I am looking forward to seeing her again soon. It is wonderful to have a new friend.

Sakriel

As Sakriel steps up into the carriage after helping his sister in and loading all of the packages, he glances back at Orion as the small man closes the carriage door. When their eyes meet, they convey their thoughts to each other without words.

Orion climbs back up in his seat, letting his eyes rest on the doorway of Halia's shop briefly before steering the horses from the curb.

Inside the carriage, Sakriel smiles, taking in the serene look on his sister's face as they head for Havenwood. His inner joy for Ciran's happiness is waging a war with the sorrow he feels for what is to be placed before her. Everything is happening so fast and time is not wasting a moment in setting things in motion.

You will not be alone, little one, he sighs inwardly. *You will not be alone.*

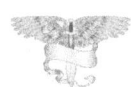

"They will look beautiful on you," Sakriel comments, watching Ciran hang up her new robes. He sits on the edge of the bed, breathing in the sweet scent of the room. The mixture of orchid and jasmine is definitely Ciran, and he has come to know it well.

"I am grateful for Halia's help in choosing them," Ciran says. She sits down beside her brother.

"You are very taken with her," he states, smiling slightly.

"She seems like a good person. I look forward to getting to know her." She sighs, looking at him. "I don't know what it is, but there is just something about her that makes me feel like we could be great friends."

Sakriel brushes a lock of hair from her face. "You don't have many of those, I know." He smiles. "But Orion and I are not so bad, are we?"

She grins. "Oh, I suppose not." Her voice is teasing. "You know you and Orion mean the world to me. Oh . . ." She suddenly jumps up and grabs a small package from the dresser, handing it to him.

Sakriel's eyes widen surprise. "You did not need to buy me anything, little one."

"I know," she says, her voice soft. "I just wanted to."

Sakriel opens the small box. As he lifts the gold chain from the cushion of cotton, his knowing eyes meet hers.

"When I was in your room last week, I noticed the chain was broken on your pendant when you took it from your drawer. The moment I saw this one in the shop I knew I had to get it for you." Ciran pauses, smiling. "It isn't much, but I wanted to give you something to let you know how much joy you have brought to me and how grateful I am to have you as my brother."

Sakriel swallows hard against the emotion in his throat, meeting her teary gaze with his own. "You could not have given me a better gift, little one. It was most thoughtful. Thank you."

"You are welcome. I have something for Orion as well. I shall give it to him when we meet for our evening meal."

"That sounds like an excellent idea," Sakriel agrees. Walking over to the window, he quietly gazes out into the distance. Taking in the view, he can understand how Ciran's memories of Krisandor would be triggered by the sight. It isn't as glorious as their home, but he can't deny its beauty.

Sadly, the beauty of this kingdom is fading. Sakriel can see it. Evil is abounding and the season of change is closer than anyone knows, with the exception of himself, Orion, and a chosen few who have been sent at this time for the coming war that will seal the fate of those who chose to remain faithful to Ubal, which is almost everyone. Only a small number have finished their journey and returned to Krisandor. Ubal's influence, as well as the dark lords before him, had been strong, and most were too weak to resist.

Sakriel's sister is one of the last to take the journey, and Ubal's anger and hatred for her because of her resistance is kindled with a fury Sakriel has never witnessed before. He wishes he could tell Ciran what is to come, but it is not his place. His father had instructed him in what he could and could not say. When the time comes, that knowledge will be revealed to her. Right now all he can do is try to prepare her.

When Ciran hears him sigh, she goes to him. "Is something wrong?" she asks, smoothing his furrowed brow with her fingers.

Sakriel turns to her, taking her hand, squeezing it gently. "Promise me, little one, that you will be careful. It is only a matter of time before you will have to face Ubal again. I don't mean to cause you worry, but I need you to be on your guard. He will use others to get to you as well. He has before and he will again."

Ciran's own brow furrows as well. "Is it so important to him to break me?"

"I am afraid it is."

"But why? I do not understand."

Sakriel hesitates, thinking about what he *can* tell her. It is still difficult for him not to share all he knows. He ponders another a moment before answering. "Because you are my flesh and blood, and we are our father's children. He has a hatred for Father that goes back to the beginning of this season when Father was here." He stared into her eyes intently. "All I can tell you, little one, is that he knows who you are. He failed with me, and he is determined not to fail with you." He embraces her, resting his chin against her brow. "I can tell you no more now."

The conversation with Sakriel stays with me throughout our meal. There is so much I still don't know and I feel unprepared and confused, yet I also feel a small sense of peace, as if something inside me knows everything will be all right.

I smile at Orion as he examines the book of poetry I have just given him. He is very pleased and tells me it is a most perfect gift. Sakriel and I listen as he reads a few lines to us, his love for the written word evident in his expression, as well as the tone of his voice.

Where light resides, darkness fades,
never again to grace the surface

where newness has permanently dawned.

Orion closes the book and smiles. I see something tangible pass between the two men before they turn their eyes to me. Sakriel says nothing, he just squeezes my hand.

"It is a most wonderful gift," Orion declares, his gentle voice breaking the silence around us.

"I am pleased it brings you so much joy."

"Now," he says, laying the book aside, "what shall we do this evening?"

"Well, there is a play beginning after dusk in the great hall," I say. "I heard from Fallon that it is quite good."

"Then a play it will be," Sakriel agrees heartily.

We finish our dessert and begin talking of our plans for tomorrow when a server approaches our table. Sakriel, expressing his thoughts about a concert scheduled for tomorrow afternoon, stops mid sentence, looking up.

"May I bring you anything else?" the young woman asks softly.

Sakriel smiles, answering for us. "No, that will be all. Thank you."

"You are welcome," she says shyly, lowering her eyes. She starts loading the large tray with empty dishes.

I watch my brother intently watching the young woman, his eyes never leaving her face. Then I take a moment to observe the girl as well. Her dark brown hair is pulled back from her face, the spiraled ringlets cascading down her back. Her lovely blue eyes are shaded by long dark lashes. I notice her repeatedly adjusting the sleeve of her robe, obviously trying to cover a brand. I can definitely understand and relate. I know all too well the shame she must be feeling.

Watching her, I am deeply moved by the sorrow and sadness in her eyes. I have never witnessed either of those things in others who are branded, and I long to put my arms around her and tell her it will be all right.

After loading everything onto the tray, the young woman smiles and says, "It has been a pleasure."

"Thank you for serving us," I say. "Perhaps one morning I might have the opportunity to serve you during my shift."

A wide smile breaks over her face. "I thought I recognized you. I have only seen you a couple of times in passing."

"Really?" I am surprised. "I am sorry. I don't remember seeing you."

"That is all right."

"My name is Ciran."

"I am Jara."

"It is a pleasure to meet you, Jara. Now that I have met you, I feel like I already know you."

Jara smiles. "That's funny. I was about to say the same thing about you."

"Are you new to Havenwood?"

"I have been here for a month, but I have always worked in the kitchen. One of the morning servers moved away and I took her place."

Sakriel smiles up at her. "Well, we are fortunate you were given our table."

Jara's cheeks color and she looks down shyly. "The fortune has been mine."

Orion and I glance at each other across the table and smile as we watch this exchange. My brother is finally showing some interest in someone. When I asked Sakriel on the day he came if he had a wife in Krisandor waiting for him, he said no, and I wondered how that could be. I supposed he would have found a mate during his own journey, but he hadn't. Now, as I observe him and Jara, I know why.

Jara turns to take the tray to the kitchen.

"Wait," Sakriel says. Jara turns back to him and he stands. "We are planning to see a play in the great hall tonight. Would you care to join us?"

Her cheeks flush as she lifts her eyes to his. "I don't know . . ." She nervously pulls on her robe sleeve with her free hand, then lowers her eyes again and I literally feel her pain.

"I would really be pleased if you accompanied us," Sakriel says, his voice gentle.

Jara raises her eyes to his once more, hesitating to answer. She swallows hard. "If I can finish in time . . . I would love to."

Sakriel smiles. "Then we shall wait for you."

Smiling, she nods before taking the tray to the kitchen.

I turn to my brother as he sits down. When his eyes meet mine, I glimpse in his the answer to my question before I even voice it. "She is the one?"

"Yes," he answers, sighing deeply. "She does not remember me, but I know her, better than anyone."

"Did *I* know her?" I ask, pondering the unexplainable connection I feel to her.

"Yes, you did. She left Krisandor a short while before I did this time." His gaze grows distant. "We played together as children and remained close through the years. Before she left, I made my feelings known to her. Because she had to leave, we could not marry, but I promised her I would find her, and I knew I would be able to keep that promise because I would be gifted with my memory this time."

Smiling tearfully, my eyes move to Orion. "You rescued

her from Ubal."

"I did, fair Ciran. She is also a strong one and I knew her purpose here as well. She resisted Ubal just as you did."

"And you will heal her?" I ask my brother.

"Yes, little one. She is still fair." His gaze moves to the kitchen doors. "And she owns my heart."

I wipe the tears slipping down my face. "How I envy you."

Sakriel doesn't ask why and I know *he* knows the reason. He reaches for my hand, holding it gently in his. "I promise you, little one, you will know the one who owns your heart when you see him."

I nod, trying to hold on to his promise. With all my heart I want to believe it.

Glancing at Orion, I cannot help thinking about him also being alone. "What about you, Orion?" I ask softly. "Is there someone for you here or in Krisandor?"

Orion

Orion is thoughtful a moment, allowing his mind to drift back to the day he and others of his kind took an oath to take upon themselves the role of guardians until they were no longer needed. That time is soon approaching. He knows well the importance of the work he vowed to perform, and he will be alone while in this position, but he still feels privileged. He also knows the worst is yet to come before it is finished.

"My time will come, Ciran," he finally says. "When my work is done and we are all again in Krisandor, my heart will be completed as well."

Barefoot, the beautiful couple walk hand in hand along the shoreline. The sand is warm between their toes and the gentle breeze is cool on their skin. The cry of seagulls can be heard as they swoop into the ocean waves and back out, soaring up into the sky again, their bodies graceful as they perform their acrobatic feats. In the distance, dolphins can be seen leaping up through the froth of the rippling blue water.

The sun shines down upon the couple, making his fair hair shimmer like spun gold and her long black waves shine like a raven's breast. The two stop and sit on a large rock side by side, watching the foaming waves roll inward, washing treasures of sand dollars and seashells ashore.

He holds her hand in his and she watches him gently trace one of the lines running over her palm with his finger. She takes in the veins beneath the lightly-tanned skin of his hands, letting her eyes travel up his muscular arms. She studies his bowed head intently, watching the breeze gently lift the golden locks falling softly against his handsome brow. She memorizes his every feature–his smooth skin, the chiseled angle of his cheeks, his full lashes. Then he lifts his deep blue gaze to hers and she becomes lost in its depths.

"I must speak with your father," he says softly, his deep voice gentle, yet powerful.

"I know."

"You know my heart, beloved."

"As you know mine."

He presses a hand to her cheek, caressing her skin for a moment before leaning in to kiss her. Just as his lips are about to touch hers, multiple giggles erupt behind them. They both turn and smile at the three small children hiding behind the rock.

"We have spies, I see." His voice is rich with amusement.

"We are not spies," the oldest of the three says. "We only wanted to walk with you."

"Did you now?" he teases. "Well, how can that be

accomplished behind a rock?"

The children smile at each other mischievously. "We did not want to interrupt. That would have been impolite."

The couple look at the children and laugh softly.

"It would indeed," the woman agrees, brushing the hair back from her face.

The man stands and takes her hand in his. "Come, Ciran," he croons softly. "Come, my beloved."

Once again I awaken as tears stream back into my hair, and I again bury the pain inside my heart. The dream is more frequent now, sometimes even staying with me during my waking moments, making it as real to me as my own name—making *him* real to me. Part of me believes it is more a memory than a dream. The other part of me is convinced it is just wishful thinking. If only I could be certain . . .

Ten

Broken Trust

I thoroughly enjoy my meal with Halia. We talk and laugh much, and I find the lovely woman to be witty and charming, so carefree and full of life. I discover that Halia has always been alone. She has no family, yet she is happy and never lets anything get her down. She has an easy laugh and a wonderful sense of humor that draws me to her, and by the end of the meal I feel as if I have always known her.

After our visit, we wait by the large front doors for Halia's carriage to arrive.

"I don't think I have ever laughed so much," Halia tells me. "Thank you for a wonderful evening."

"I am so glad we could do this. I cannot remember ever enjoying a meal more."

"We shall have to meet again." Halia pauses. "As a matter of fact, I have some free time tomorrow. Do you have plans?"

"No, I don't," I answer, excited at the prospect of visiting with her again. Orion will be out most of the afternoon and evening, and Sakriel has plans with Jara.

I can't help smiling as I think on the ceremony held two days ago that bound Sakriel and Jara together as husband and wife. They make a striking couple and I am very happy for my brother, but I am a little envious, too. Chastising myself, I mentally push the selfish feelings aside. My time will come one day. I am truly overjoyed for them both. Halia draws me from my thoughts.

"I will send my carriage for you and we can dine at my home. It is a humble place but comfortable. Please say yes."

"I would be delighted," I answer without hesitation.

"Wonderful! Then I shall see you tomorrow evening." She gives my hand a squeezed. "I am so glad we are friends, fair Ciran."

"I am as well," I say, returning the squeeze.

Halia's carriage finally arrives. The driver jumps down, tips his hat to me, and helps her into the carriage.

I waved as she rides away, anticipating tomorrow evening. I decide that as far as the friendship department goes, things are starting to look up.

Sakriel

"Where is she?" Sakriel asks Orion the following evening. He and Jara had gone to Ciran's room to invite her to dine with them. When there was no answer, he had immediately gone in search of Orion. The small man is just coming back from the stable, having brushed down the horses and settling them for the evening.

Orion places a calming hand on Sakriel's arm. "She made no mention to me of her plans this evening, but wherever she is, I am sure she is fine."

Deep down Sakriel knows where his sister is, and he knew Orion does as well. "How can you be so sure, with Ubal out there waiting for another chance to claim her?" The last part of the question causes Jara to shiver, and he senses her remembering her encounter with the dark lord. He gives her hand a gentle squeeze.

"I am not sure," Orion says. "But we can only hope."

When Orion looks up, Sakriel reads the answer to his

unvoiced question in the small man's eyes.

Yes, Orin relays to him silently. *She will know the truth about Halia soon enough.*

Jara squeezes Sakriel's hand. "Let us go and have our dinner. I am sure your sister will be back soon."

Sakriel smiles, kissing her hand, grateful to have her by his side. "I am sure you're right." For his wife's sake he does his best to put his fears aside for the moment.

Isiral

Gazing through the dining hall window of Fairmoor out into the distance, Isiral takes a bite of the warm, fluffy bread and silently ponders the insistent restlessness consuming him. His blue eyes intently take in the scene outside the widow.

There are gardeners trimming a long row of bushes at the edge of the green lawn. Two others are pruning the trees. As short as the men are, Isiral doesn't know how they are able to reach high enough to complete the job, but they do. Hamlet says it is a secret ability that is gifted only to them, for they are guardians, possessing great and powerful gifts.

Isiral smiles as he thinks of Hamlet. From the moment the small man picked him up in the town square, he felt a kinship toward him. He has spent many an hour with Hamlet, discussing Krisandor and the memories they both have of their home. True, this part of the world holds beauty, but it is slowly fading. He can see it all around him. Krisandor, however, exudes a splendor that defies description. He misses it very much.

Resting his chin on a closed fist, Isiral continues to contemplate. This part of his journey has been one of waiting and observing the human heart, both its weaknesses and its strengths. What he has witnessed so far saddens him. Despite the beauty all around him, evil abounds like a sickness. Men fight, steal from, and cheat other men. Greed cankers the soul and right is sacrificed for wrong. For the most part, people wear their brands proudly like a medal they have won–like some kind of reward for their choices and actions. Ubal's reach knows no limits.

Thinking on his own encounter with the vile creature, Isiral's powerful hands involuntarily form fists against the wooden table. True, he has resisted Ubal's powers, but he knows what the monster is capable of. He must be stopped, and Isiral understands that this is one of the major purposes of his journey.

Yes, he is ready to help in the task, and had prepared himself the best he could. It is only a matter of time.

"Your home is very lovely," I say to Halia as we exit through the back door of her cottage. The meal had been delicious and filling, and they decide to take a stroll through the garden and work off some of the food.

"I have never seen so many lovely flowers."

"Thank you," Halia says, a pleased smile curving her lips. "I love variety, so I usually plant as many types of flowers as I can. I just love beautiful things."

"As do I." I close my eyes and breathe in the intoxicating mixture of scents in the air. The perfume of roses, lilies, lilacs, lavender, and jasmine is circulated by the gentle breeze blowing through the garden.

"Occasionally, I take a few cuttings to town and sell them at the shop. Most of my customers are men. They buy them for their wives, their true loves, or sometimes even their mistresses."

I arch a brow at the last comment.

"Usually the men are trying to impress or make up for one thing or another. There is always an ulterior motive. Nothing is ever as it seems . . ." Halia's voice trails off.

Noticing the distant look in her eyes, I ask, "Are you all

right?"

She quickly smiles. "I am fine, just a little tired."

"Perhaps I should leave and let you get some rest."

"No, please stay. I will be fine. I do so enjoy your company."

"I enjoy yours as well."

We continue to look at the flowers. Halia slowly strolls to the edge of the garden and her eyes move to the bordering forest.

"I would like to show you something, Ciran. I have a special place that I go to when I just want to get away from the world. A place that no one knows about. I would like to share it with you."

"I would love to see it," I say, flattered that she thinks enough of me to share a private part of herself.

Halia gestures for me to follow her and we enter the forest. I am awed by the beauty of the trees. Some of them look to be old, as if they have been here since the beginning of time. Each seems to take on a personality of its own and each is uniquely shaped.

Dried leaves crackle beneath my feet as we walk, and the gentle wind stirring the trees gradually becomes stronger the deeper we go into the forest. The same breeze blows back wisps of hair that have escaped the bun at the back of my head. I am surprised that there are no signs of wildlife–no birds, chipmunks, squirrels, rabbits, raccoons, or any other animals. It is like the whole area has been abandoned.

Soon the weather turns colder, taking me by surprise. I rub my arms against the chill.

Halia glances back at me as my step slows. "Do not be afraid, Ciran," she says softly. "It is not much further."

Part of me really is afraid and I want to turn back, but another part wants to trust Halia. After all, the woman has given me no reason to distrust her. Taking a deep breath, I continue to follow her, hoping we reach our destination soon.

"Ah, there it is," Halia says, pointing ahead.

My eyes widen in surprise when Halia's secret place comes into view. I hadn't known what to expect, but I definitely wasn't expecting this.

The building is gray and about the size of Halia's cottage. It looks like a miniature castle. The two front windows are stained glass and the outside stone walls are draped in ivory and moss. It is beautiful. A light glows through the windows, beckoning to weary travelers. And by the time we reach the front door, I *feel* like a weary traveler.

"I can't wait for you to see the inside," Halia tells me as she pulls a key from the pocket of her robe. She sticks it in the old lock and turns until it clicks. Then she turns back to me, her smile fading slightly.

"Are you ready?"

"Yes," I answer, but before I can wonder about the change in Halia's expression, she again smiles warmly.

She hesitates another moment before pushing the metal door open. The hinges squeak loudly and eeriness creeps into me. As we slowly enter the dimly lit foyer, I am chilled even more by a sudden cold draft.

I glance at the paintings lining the stone walls, but because the lighting so dim I can't make out many details.

Halia stops at a set of double doors on the right. "It will be much warmer in this room," she says, giving me a weak smile.

I return her smile and try to discern the wariness coming over me. She opens the doors, gesturing for me to go in. Hesitantly, I enter the room. However, as soon as I do, I experience a sensation that causes the very hairs on the back of my neck to stand up. Turning to my right, I freeze.

"Hello, fair Ciran," Ubal says, lounging in a large, black leather chair in the corner. His smile is wide. "At last, we meet again."

Isiral

It is midnight when Isiral is awakened by a firm knock on his bedroom door. He had only fallen asleep five minutes before because he hadn't been able to turn his thoughts off. His mind is forever going in a million different directions and his restlessness is growing more every day.

Running a rough hand through his tousled hair, he quickly puts on his robe and heads to the door, wondering who could be stopping by at this hour. As soon as he opens the door and his eyes meet those of the person standing before him, his heart begins to race.

He knows this man! He can't remember how, but he knows him. Isiral takes in the man's beautiful face and searches his mind, trying to remember exactly how he knows him. Then the man extends his hand and Isiral clasps it firmly.

"Come, Isiral," Sakriel says softly. "It is time."

Eleven

Courage

Emotional shudders wrack my body and I blink hot tears onto my face, amazed that I still have tears left.

Hours. It has been hours since Halia lured me into Ubal's hands. Hours since the vile creature had imprisoned me in this cell of a room, but it seems like days.

Leaning back in the cushioned chair, I struggle to wipe my tears. My hands are tightly bound, as well as my feet, and the ropes cut into my skin, causing drops of blood to stain my gown. Even if I could untie myself, I couldn't escape. The heavy metal door is locked from the outside and there are no windows in the cold damp room. The only furniture is the chair I sit in, a small bed, and a table with a lamp. The gray stone walls are bare and the floor is covered in dirt. It is the bleakest room I have ever seen. For now, it is indeed my prison.

Relaxing deeper into the cushion, I close my eyes and mentally review the events that find me in this situation.

As soon as Ubal makes his presence known, Halia locks the door. I turn to her, shock stunning my body. "How could you do this?" I cry. "You were supposed to be my friend! I trusted you!"

Halia's eyes are sad. "You should not have trusted me." Her voice is low, forlorn, resigned, but I don't care.

I turn back to Ubal. By now he is only inches away from me. Squaring my shoulders I face him fully. I know I have to be brave. Ubal thrives on a person's fear and I am not going to give him the satisfaction of seeing mine. I will not cower to him.

"It does not matter what you do to me," I finally say. "I will not give in to you. You will not break me."

Ubal smiles, his brow rising slightly. "Really? Do you really think you are still strong enough to resist me? Well, let me explain something to you, my dear Ciran. In case you did not know, no one knows where you are, and I have all the time in the world. One way or another, you will be mine."

"This is about my father, is it not?" My voice is calm. "I know you hate him."

"You don't know anything!" he roars, taking me by surprise. "You have absolutely no idea what our history is!"

"No, I do not know much about your relationship with my father," I continue to speak calmly, though my heart is threatening to beat through my chest. "I don't really remember my father, and I only know what my brother has told me. But I do know you hate him."

"Oh, yes, your brother, Sakriel." He laughs bitterly. "I should have known he would come back. The brat just couldn't stay away, could he? Told you about our history, did he?"

"Only bits of it," I answer, very sure I am about to hear more of it, tainted by Ubal's thinking, of course.

"Well, pull up a chair, fair Ciran," he says bitterly, taking my arm, yanking me across the room to the leather chair. He looks at my wrist where the brand had been, his eyes showing surprise. "It seems you really are fair again. I don't know how you managed to get rid of my mark, but you will not stay unbranded for long." He thrusts me into the chair. Then he smiles at Halia. "I am about to tell a wonderful bedtime story, my dear. You should take a seat as

well. After all, you do so love my stories, do you not?"

Halia averts her eyes and sits in a chair a few feet away from me. I am still so hurt and angered by her actions, I can't even look at her. I had really believed the woman was my friend. I thought there was finally someone besides Sakriel and Orion that I could trust. I was sorely mistaken.

Ubal turns his attention back to me. "Now, where was I? Oh, yes. Once upon a time . . ." He stops, releasing a bitter chuckle. "Oh, this is too rich."

I stare, thinking he has truly gone mad. He is acting like a madman. Staring at the handsome face he is wearing now, it isn't hard at all to remember what he really looks like. He can hide his true face in front of others, but it will always be there, burning behind the facade he displays. He is very good at the art of illusion.

I watch his eyes narrow, as if he is reading my thoughts.

"I didn't always hate your father, you know? Once upon a time he was a great friend to me, and I loved him like a brother." I don't try to hide my skepticism. "I know you don't believe that, but I did. We were that close. We had so much power, he and I. We were determined to save the world. Or rather, I was. Cillian's idea of saving the world was to let everyone continue to choose for themselves. Can you believe that?" His expression is incredulous. "I thought this world

had been disposed of radicals. I had made sure of that. Amusingly, portraits of some of those weaklings are displayed in the dining hall at Havenwood. No doubt you have wondered about those paintings."

He is right. I have been curious. I choose not to comment, but my eyes do widen slightly as my questions about the men are suddenly answered.

"They look larger than life, but I can assure you they were small men when it came to the things that counted." He laughs. "They were even smaller once they lost their heads." He laughs again. "A private joke. Anyway," he goes on, "I thought I had rid the world of free-thinking radicals, and there I was, friends with one."

His voice turns hard. "Having the dark lords take over was one of the best things that could ever happen to this part of the world. But did you know they were not always dark? It wasn't until they began to be corrupted by power that they changed. And when that change happened, I wanted to be a part of it, only I would use the power to make things better, and the people would love me for it. Those pitiful excuses for men had no real idea what to do with all the power they possessed. But I did. So one by one I took it from them and harnessed it until I have now become the most powerful being to ever grace this world. I guess you could say my *power shows in my outward appearance at times, eh?" His lip curls up in a sneer. "Somehow your father gained power, enough power to build a new kingdom on the other side of this one, and the only way a person can be privileged enough to permanently live in his kingdom is if they can endure a so-called journey here. What a joke that was. I've branded so many people, I'm sure Krisandor must be fairly empty. Most never make it back because they realize where true happiness lies, which is here, in my kingdom. Men don't want freedom of choice, they want leadership, someone to mold them, shape them, dictate to them.*

"So, fair Ciran, winning your soul will be my revenge against your father. I wanted Sakriel as well, but you will do."

Shaking my head, I shoot him a pathetic look. "You seek retribution for a supposed wrong that was never done to you."

"You are absolutely right, only it was not supposed. Cillian claimed power that was not his to claim. It should be mine. All of it. And I will have that retribution if it is the last thing I do." Ubal flashes a smug smile, and then pauses in his speech, resting his evil gaze on Halia. "Do you have anything you wish to add, my dear?"

Halia closes her eyes and looks away, but not before I

see the tears in them.

"Hmmm. I thought not." Ubal walks over to a small table and picks up a goblet of the forbidden red liquid. He then approaches me. "Why don't you drink this?" he says, holding out the goblet. "It will clear your head and give you some clarity."

"I will not." My voice is vehement. "And I will not give in to you!"

Ubal smiles, sipping from the goblet. "Oh, you will. It is only a matter of time. You are not as strong as you think you are." He moves closer, reaching out to touch my face and I draw back before his fingers make contact with my skin.

"Yes," Ubal says, his evil smile growing, "it is only a matter of time before you break.."

Pulling my thoughts to the present, I sniff as my eyes again move around the cold room. I close them and sigh, knowing I must be strong. I must stay true and not weaken. It is only a matter of time before Sakriel and Orion find me. I have to hold on.

"Give me strength," I whisper into the silence.

Ubal pours himself another goblet of Splendorfire. Raising his glass to Halia, he smiles. "What's the matter, my dear? Have you grown weary of my little garden party already?"

Halia looks at Ubal, her eyes expressing a mixture of sadness and disdain. "I did not know it would be like this."

"Well, what did you expect?" Ubal says with a laugh. "You had to know from the beginning that sooner or later you would have to get your hands dirty."

"Yes, but most of us choose this life. She has not."

"Well, when has that ever mattered?"

"It has always mattered."

"Not to me. But why am I even saying this? You already know that. You have always known. I always win."

Halia smiles slightly. "Not with Sakriel," she says softly. "And you will not with Ciran, either."

Ubal slams the goblet on the table, sloshing its contents on the dark wood as he takes in her smug expression. "You are enjoying this, aren't you?"

"How could I not?"

"She is weak!" he roars, shaking his fist in Halia's face, causing her to flinch. "And mark my words. Before this night is over I will own her, and then I will take advantage of the weakness her loss will create in Cillian, and I will crush him

161

and his kingdom."

Halia

Halia straightens and faces him fully, her eyes flashing bravely. She is tired. Tired of all of it. The scaly skin on her back itches as she thinks back on her own weaknesses and the choices she made that find her here in such a hopeless predicament. Once upon a time she had everything. A wonderful life, true friends, and family. She once radiated with the same light she sees in Ciran. She had studied the scroll diligently and lived by it, and she had been fair, unspoiled and untouched by evil.

All of that changed when she met Ubal. She became blinded, deceived. She had become so lost, she betrayed those closest to her. Taken in by Ubal's web of deceit, his promises of making everything easier, she lost everything. She well remembers the day Ubal became the new and only dark lord after killing the last three. She had been blinded by his power and his assurances that his way was the right way, that his world would be a perfect world. As long as people submitted to his will, it did seem perfect. When Cillian left and many followed after him, Ubal wished them good riddance and assumed he would never see any of those people again.

Cillian began sending the grown children of these people back to be tested. Halia remembers Ubal laughing hysterically when they all started showing up with no memory of who they were before leaving their own world. He swore he would own them all. A few were able to make it back to Krisandor unbranded. Only a few. But only after Sakriel had come for his journey and showed them it was possible. Because of Ubal's failure, he has been in a rage ever since, preying upon every weakness he can find, just waiting for the day Ciran would begin her journey.

Halia heaves a sorrowful sigh. With everything that has happened, with all the evil acts she has assisted in over the years, she knows it is too late for her. She is trapped and there is no way out. But it isn't too late for Ciran. Halia can only hope Ubal will fail at his attempt to break the young woman.

"I am finished," she finally says. "I will help you no longer."

"Who do you think you are talking to, woman?" he snarls, his appearance changing to his true self He thrusts his hideously-scaly face in hers. "I own you. You owe your very life to me, as pitiful as it may be!" He moves back slightly.

"Yes, you will help me. Things are starting to happen quickly, but my plan will be carried out. I have many people on my side, many who have caught on to my vision. We have a lot of work ahead of us, but by the time I am done, Cillian and his kingdom will be but a memory."

Halia stares at him, her eyes narrowing as she begins to grasp what he is saying. "You plan to destroy Krisandor. But I thought you only wanted power over the people here."

Ubal chuckles. "Well, with your finite mind you would think that, wouldn't you? No, my dear, I will not stop until I have everyone in my power, which means naturally I will have to go after the ones that got away."

"Your plan is insane! You will never get through the gate."

"Oh, I will not only get through it, I will destroy it, and you are going to help me. You are, after all, the perfect person to help me. The logical choice, do you not agree?"

Halia presses her tight fists to her sides. "I will not help you," she says with quiet vehemence.

"Then perhaps I shall have to give you some time to think about it." He grabs her arm, pulling her from the room, down the dimly-lit hall. When he reaches the metal door, he takes a key from the pocket of his robe and unlocks the door.

Hearing the lock turning on the door startles me. I keep her eyes fixed as it creaks open. In the next instant, Halia is shoved into the room, and unable to steady herself, she lands on the dirt-covered floor.

"I brought you some company," Ubal says, his smile twisted. "I'm sure you two have much to talk about. I will leave you alone to talk some sense into each other because neither of you are leaving until we all have a mutual understanding." He smiles again. "Oh, Ciran," he adds just before closing the door, "if you are thirsty and need refreshment, I have just the thing. You need only ask." He grins and closes the door, locking it behind him.

I watch Halia stand and brush the dirt from her robe, wondering what she has done to incur Ubal's wrath when mere hours before she was his cohort. *And why has he put them in the same room?*

Halia moves to the bed and says, "We are supposed to talk some sense into each other."

"What is that supposed to mean?" I ask curtly, far past being in the mood to be cordial.

"Well," she says with a sigh, "I am supposed to try and convince you to give in to Ubal because his way is the only way, and you are meant to try and convince me to continue helping him in his insane quest to have total power over the world."

"Why does he need the latter? I thought you *were* helping him."

"That was before," she says softly. "I told him I will not help him any longer, so he has decided to hold me prisoner here as well until I come to my senses." She looks up at me, her eyes sad. "I have been blinded for many years, seduced by his lies. Only now have I come to understand the truth, and that truth is Ubal cares for no one. He is pure evil and only wants one thing—to make us all slaves to his will. He will stop at nothing until he has reached that goal."

"Why are you saying all this? Is it to gain my trust, because if it is, that will not happen."

"I am saying it because it is true, and also because . . . I need your forgiveness. I hate myself for what I have done to you, and to so many others. I hate myself for my part in all of this. I have been under Ubal's control since the beginning of his reign as dark lord and have done many unspeakable things that I shall never be able to make up for."

Halia pauses, wiping at a sudden tear, and I see genuine emotion in her eyes.

"I know it is too late for me," she continues, "for I am surely trapped in this life and in Ubal's world, but I will do everything in my power to right the wrong I have done to you. In return I only ask for your forgiveness."

I don't know how or why, but my heart softens toward her. Even after the betrayal and hurt, I feel an unexplainable compassion. Maybe it is the fact that we are both trapped in this situation with a small hope of being found and only have each other to look to for support. I honestly don't know. However, I *do* know it would be wrong to hold onto anger. Somewhere, sometime in my life, a gentle voice taught me these words: *Anger is not the way.*

"I do forgive you," I finally say. "I don't know how this will all turn out, but I hold no anger against you."

Halia smiles, another tear trailing down her pale cheek. "Thank you," she whispers. She sniffs, wiping her face. "Now," she says, standing and approaching me, "let us see about getting these ropes untied."

Twelve

The Rescue

The dawning of the next morning finds Sakriel, Orion, Isiral, and eight other men quietly moving through the dark woods behind Halia's cottage. The sky is overcast, and the surrounding vegetation is lightly sprinkled with morning dew. The forest is silent, devoid of wildlife in this part. The dry leaves barely crackle beneath the feet of the men as they walk, so soft and sure are their steps.

They are all dressed in leather leggings, billowy off-white shirts topped with leather vests, and high boots. Each has a sword at his waist. It had taken all night to gather what men they have. Sadly, they were the only unbranded men to be found. Ubal's evil is far-reaching and covers all of the Kingdom he now calls Jubilus, which leads Sakriel to believe the final days of the season are definitely upon them. Ubal has begun to gather his troops, assuming he will be victorious. Why else would he choose to name the land now?

Before they reach the small stone building, Sakriel signals for the men to pause, and sends one ahead to scout for any of Ubal's men around the building. He knows Ubal would never leave the place unguarded. While he waits, Sakriel closes his eyes, mentally attempting to send comfort to his sister. He tries to imagine what Ciran has been through, but the images of his mind only breed anger, so he clears them away and concentrates on reaching his sister through thought.

All will be well, little one, he breathes inwardly. *All will be well.*

As they waited among the trees, Isiral's heart begins to experience an ache he has never felt before. It defies all explanation. It is as if he can feel the pain of the young woman being held captive, and the urge to just charge in and take her away is so strong, it threatens to tear his very insides apart. Beads of perspiration form on his forehead as his heart, will and mind begin to battle with one another. He must calm himself. If he doesn't, he will blow everything, and in doing so, she will be lost to them.

Closing his eyes, he concentrates on the vision he had of her last night, and again this morning. A vision of her standing with him by the moss-covered gate of Krisandor– her gentle, tear-filled emerald eyes looking up at him through long, dark lashes that matched the shimmering waves of her hair, her golden skin that felt so smooth beneath his fingertips, and her arms that felt so warm as she wrapped them around him.

Yes, he remembers his beloved now. His Ciran. He remembers her more clearly than anyone or anything else. He wonders why this is. Why have the memories been thrust upon his mind this way? He has no answers. He only knows he has to keep his wits about him. He must lock the emotions away until it is time to release them.

So with one final moment of deep concentration, Isiral speaks to Ciran through his heart.

Let your heart and mind be at ease, for I am here, my beloved. And soon you will be safe in my arms.

Halia

Halia is sitting in the chair watching Ciran resting on the bed. They have been given no water and are both worn and weary. They have no idea of the time or even if it is daylight yet. With no windows and four stone walls to stare at, keeping track of time is impossible. It is also irrelevant. What matters is survival. True, Halia worries for her own safety, but she worries for Ciran's even more. She hopes with everything in her that help will arrive soon.

Pressing her face in her hands and swallowing against fresh emotion rising inside her, Halia is startled by Ciran's soft gasp. She jumps up, hurrying to her side. "What is it?" she whispers, sitting on the edge of the bed, pressing a hand to her cheek.

Opening my eyes, I stare up at the cracked ceiling as tears roll back into my hair. I press a hand to my chest and smile as the vision of the beautiful fair-haired man with deep-blue eyes again makes itself known to me. His gentle voice still fills my mind, surrounding me in a comforting warmth that is beyond description.

I am here, beloved, he had said. *And soon you will be safe in my arms.*

"Everything will be fine," I finally say, looking at Halia. Taking in her worried expression, I smile. "Sakriel is near, and he has brought help. We will be rescued."

"How do you know this?" Halia asks, her expression both perplexed and hopeful.

I squeeze her hand. "I just know."

Sakriel and the rest of the men are alert when their man returns with a report.

"How many?" Sakriel asks as the stocky man wipes a sweaty palm against his thigh. He leans over to catch his breath.

"Nine, all of them big, but sluggish in movement."

Orion makes a low noise in his throat. "No doubt they are all experiencing the effects of too much Splendorfire from last night."

"Dumb oafs," another man mutters.

"I agree," Isiral adds. "But that shall be to our favor."

Sakriel nods, sensing Isiral's anxiousness over Ciran, though he hides it well. "It shall." He bids all the men to come closer. "All right, this is the plan."

"What's this?" one of the four branded men snarls as Sakriel and three of his men approach the front of the house. Those words are the only ones spoken. In the next second, the only sound is the clashing of swords.

Around the back, the situation is similar as Orion and two warriors charge the three men standing guard. The same is happening on the side as Isiral outmatches the men blade for blade.

Each man remembers Sakriel's admonition: Do not take a life unless it is absolutely necessary. They are all able to keep that charge. With each man putting down one of Ubal's, and Isiral disabling two, the fighting lasts for less than a minute. Sakriel's men sustain no major injuries and are all in good shape. Of course, they know the small victory is due in part to the lingering effects of Splendorfire on the enemy, but they are grateful.

Unpacking the ropes they brought, they secure Ubal's men. The other men stand guard while Sakriel, Orion, and

Isiral cautiously enter the building.

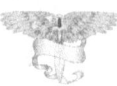

Isiral

Isiral's anxiousness increases. They search each room, but there is no sign of Ubal. He shakes his head, half amused. Apparently Ubal left the guards in charge, and what a pitiful excuse they were. He is sure the men will lose their heads when their master returns and finds his prize gone.

Continuing their search, they discover every door is unlocked except one.

As Sakriel and Orion break the lock with an ax and pry the door open, Isiral's heart pounds madly. He is about to see her. Somehow he can feel her presence, sense her emotions, and what he feels from her at this moment is calmness, as if she knows everything will be all right.

Isiral holds back and lets Sakriel enter first, his eyes immediately drawn to Ciran where she sits on the bed. His gaze then moves to Halia and anger immediately creases his brow. He watches Sakriel gathering his sister in his arms, reading the mixture of emotions playing across Sakriel's face and he understands.

Isiral stands with Orion just inside the doorway. He is

overjoyed to find Ciran safe, but as he continues to gaze at her, his feelings for her swell. Even in the dimly lit room her features are unmistakable. She is even more beautiful than he remembered.

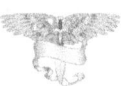

Sakriel draws back and studies my bruised wrists, anger clearly written in his expression.

I lift a hand to his face and smile. "It is all right. I am well."

"I cannot tell you how grateful I am for that," he says, squeezing my hands.

I nod, lifting my eyes to the two men standing in the doorway. My gaze settles on Isiral and my heart begins to race so fast, I can hardly breathe. My beloved is here! He has come and he is even more magnificent than my visions and dreams showed him to be. I smile at the emotion I see in his eyes as they remain fixed on mine, and I suddenly find myself longing to hear his voice, for I know its timber will be rich and his words gentle.

Halia's urgent voice cuts through my thoughts.

"We must leave," she says, standing. "There is much I must tell you."

"It appears so," Sakriel says, his eyes fixed on the older woman. "Why are you in here?"

I watch Halia bravely meet my brother's unwavering stare, and I sense something passing back and forth between them. "I told Ubal I would no longer help him and he decided to punish me as well."

"Sakriel," I softly say, "she has been a comfort to me. She is telling the truth."

Sakriel turns skeptical eyes back to Halia, and I understand his suspicion of her motives. He helps her to her feet and signals for Orion to escort her out. Taking my hand, we move to the door.

My eyes again meet those of my beloved's. I stop in front of him and it is physically painful to keep myself from reaching out to him. Now is not the time. But that time will come soon. I read in his eyes what he doesn't say and I smile, letting my own gaze lend voice to my thoughts. Then we quietly leave.

Ubal

Later, Ubal sits in the leather chair, his insides fuming. His face contorts into a look of evil rage as he thinks about

Ciran. His prize has escaped him yet again. He had used one of his most cunning means to ensnare her this time, but the young woman wouldn't break. Her will to fight him had been too strong. And now he is more angry than he has been during his entire miserable existence. Ciran is one of the few souls to resist his power during his reign as dark lord and this fact burns him from the inside out.

Ubal knows it is only a matter of time before his enemies attempt to destroy him and he knows now that Ciran will have a part in it unless he breaks her. He *must* break her because she is the key to everything now. She is his way to Cillian.

Releasing a low growl, Ubal picks up the jewel-encrusted goblet he'd sipped from earlier and hurls it across the room against the wall, his chest heaving as he watches the red liquid drip down, leaving dark streaks on the gray stone.

Lifting his fist to the sky, he angrily swears an oath to destroy Ciran's spirit. He will own her if it is the last thing he does. He will win the war to come. Jubilus is his, and Krisandor will be his as well.

Part Four
A Course Set In Stone

Thirteen

To Thwart A Plan

Sakriel

The small group of men and women sit around a large table in a room on the lower level of Havenwood. The elegant chamber is lit by a massive crystal chandelier that hangs high over the table. The stone walls are adorned with brass framed paintings of landscapes and wildlife. Most of the landscape paintings are of Havenwood's surroundings–different angles of the courtyard, the field of wildflowers out back in the distance, the gray mountains.

In attendance are Sakriel, Orion, Isiral, Halia, Jara, and the five men who assisted in Ciran's rescue. Sakriel had suggested that Ciran stay in her room and rest and she complied without protest. He promised to fill her in on the meeting later.

Everyone listens attentively as Halia tells them of her history with Ubal. A large piece of that history is left out, but Sakriel is painfully privy to that knowledge.

When Halia has finished speaking, Sakriel silently scans the faces around the table. "As you all know, the end of the season is upon us. Just as it was foretold centuries ago, the land has grown weary of trying to sustain the constant conflict of good and evil. We must use these final days to convince those who follow Ubal that his way is not the way. We need to help them see that they will never be truly happy with Ubal in control of their very lives. They have been deceived and follow him blindly. We must try and convince them of the truth. More importantly, we must help them understand that once the gate is shut, it will be sealed forever.

"You may have noticed that business at Havenwood has slowed substantially. Even the regular customers hardly frequent the establishment anymore. Ubal's arm reaches far. We have our work cut out for us."

Halia raises her hand and Sakriel gestures for her to speak.

"But Sakriel, you do not understand. Ubal is completely

mad in his thirst for power. His hatred of your father knows no bounds or limits. Not only does he want to own everyone, he plans to destroy Krisandor as well."

With her words, there are a few gasps from the group. Sakriel puts a calming hand up, looking at Halia intently. "Do you know how he plans to bring this destruction about?"

She nods, swallowing before speaking again. The weighing guilt of her part in this is clearly written on her face. "He said he will find the gate and destroy it, and then send some of his people through."

"We must not let that happen," Orion says. "Our loved ones are awaiting our return."

"It will not happen," Sakriel assures. "Ubal's jealousy and hatred of my father will destroy him before he or anyone working with him can ever set a foot in Krisandor."

"But how will you stop him?" Halia asks.

Sakriel looks at her evenly. "Do you doubt our ability to defeat him?" His voice hints of defiance that he quickly swallows back.

Halia sighs. "No, I do not doubt your abilities. It is just that I was held captive by his power for a long time and I have seen what he is capable of. The people worship him and are completely obedient to him. Any and everything Ubal asks of them, they do. They are all weak." She lowers her head, adding softly, "As I have been."

With his gaze fixed on her bowed head, Sakriel's softening grows. He feels her sorrow and can no longer doubt her sincerity. He keeps his gaze on her until she lifts her head, meeting his eyes with her own unwavering stare. She gives him a trembling smile.

Returning her smile, Sakriel says, "It seems those weaknesses are now turning into strengths."

Halia wipes the tear trailing down her face. "You mean there's a little hope for me?" she asks, her voice lightly teasing.

"More than a little," he answers.

Halia

The solemness in Sakriel's voice sobers Halia. She had not expected him to be so kind after all the wrong she has done. As far as she is concerned, her actions are unforgivable, yet in not so many words he *has* forgiven her. She asks herself how this could be. She then glances around at all the other faces in the room, all still showing various degrees of mistrust. She can't blame them really. They have no reason to trust her. This one small act of helping to stop

Ubal can never make up for all she did to help him in the first place. Still, she knows she must try. Sakriel's voice again breaks through her pondering.

Sakriel

"We must plan against the attack that is certain to come soon," he says, addressing the group. "We must ready ourselves and prepare. I must also inform Father of Ubal's plan. Then he and our people there can prepare as well. We need to try to turn some of Ubal's followers and help them to see the truth." He lets his eyes roam around the table. "It will take all of us to stop Ubal from gaining complete power."

Elan, one of the young warriors glances at Halia before speaking. "Forgive me, but are we sure the information we have been given is accurate? How can we be sure the bearer of that information can be trusted?"

Others around the table nod simultaneously, echoing Elan's question.

Sakriel watches Halia drop her eyes to the table. "Like many others, Halia was deceived. Her eyes have now been opened to the truth. She has made an enemy of Ubal and has nothing to gain by leading us astray. I believe what she has told us. And since one of the ways in which we will defeat Ubal will be by sharing the truth with those who worship him, do you not think it is fitting to start now by embracing a heart that has already changed?"

Elan and the rest of the group look at Halia, who meets their eyes with her own teary gaze. Bowing slightly, he says, "My apologies, my lady."

Halia smiles. "Apology accepted, but only if you will all forgive me for my part in all of this."

"All is forgiven." Orion's gentle voice resonates around the room.

Sakriel lays a comforting hand on her shoulder, grateful beyond words for the miracle that has occurred but knowing he cannot let the magnitude of it settle in just yet, at least not until he is alone. He glances over at Orion and sees understanding in his eyes. "Now for the plan."

Before Sakriel can say another word there is a sound in another part of the room, like a chair scraping against the stone floor. Sakriel's eyes shoot to Orion and Isiral's and the two men immediately get up.

There is definitely someone else in the room.

The three men fix stare at a large leather chair in the far corner of the room and slowly move toward it. Everyone else sits silently, waiting in suspense. The tension in the air is tangibly thick.

Just as Sakriel reaches the chair, the unseen person jumps up and trying to dodge him, but the attempt is blocked by Orion and Isiral. Sakriel picks the small man up, dropping him in the chair.

"Hemlock!" Orion booms when the guardian finally looks up. "What in heavens name are you about?"

The white-haired, bearded guardian narrows his dark eyes, replying with a sneer, "I owe you no explanation!"

Sakriel stands over the man. His voice is surprisingly calm. "You *will* tell us what evil you are up to. You aren't going anywhere, so I suggest you cooperate."

Hemlock stands, smiling at the three men. "Do you honestly think you can hold me?" He raises his arms, summoning his power as a guardian, attempting to expand his size and strength, but to his surprise, nothing happens. He closes his eyes, concentration etching his features. He raises his arms again, and again, nothing happens. Finally opens his eyes, he glances at Orion, fear clearly written on his face.

Orion shakes his head, his eyes sad. "The evil you have obtained through your bargain with Ubal must run deep." He looks at the small man with regret etched in his features. "Did you not know that once a guardian embraces evil his powers are no more?"

Hemlock's eyes widen in horror. "No!" he yells. "Ubal told me that was a lie, that I could never lose my power!"

Isiral shakes his head, scoffing loudly. "You expected a liar to tell you the truth? He would say anything to get you to help him. You of all people should know that. Good grief, man, you are a guardian!"

"You mean *were*," Orion interjects. "You have chosen a dark path. Why, Hemlock? Why have you chosen to help the very being bent on destroying everything?"

"I was sure his way was the right way," Hemlock replies, his head bowed, his countenance seemingly contrite. Then, as if someone has just flipped a switch inside him, he looks up at the three, his expression a mixture of anger and disdain. "The loss of my powers does not matter. When Ubal defeats Cillian he will set things right, and mark my words, he will be victorious."

Orion heaves a deep sigh. "I can't believe what I am hearing. What is happening? How has Ubal gained so much power that even guardians, the very elect, are deceived?"

Sakriel moves directly in front of Hemlock. There will be a time to pity this lost guardian, however, this is not that time. "We will never let you relay what you have heard here to Ubal. You know this, do you not?"

Hemlock chuckles, his tone bitter. "I *do* know, but

understand this. I will never tell you anything."

"I think you will," Sakriel says with confidence. He turns, making eye contact with the rest of the group. They are all still in their chairs, having taken the whole confrontation. Turning back to Isiral and finally Orion, he finds support in their eyes. He hates what he is about to do, but he has been left with no other choice.

"What are you doing?" the small man yells as Isiral and Orion take his arms, pinning him to the chair.

Sakriel leans down, pulling the front of Hemlock's robe open, exposing the large scaly patch of skin on his abdomen. His eyes meet the former guardian's, his expression instantly turning to stone. "After finishing my own journey I was given the gift to heal. Now . . ." He pauses a moment, placing his hand close to the brand without touching it. The small man immediately begins to writhe in pain. Sakriel watches Hemlock squeeze his eyes shut, moaning another moment before moving his hand away. "With that same gift," he continues, "I can cause pain. Not unduly, of course, but I can summon the ability when necessary, and it never has been . . . until now."

Sakriel waits, allowing Hemlock to take a deep breath, sensing his pain slowly subsiding. Beads of perspiration have formed on the man's forehead and drip down into his eyes.

He looks up at Sakriel, his expression hard once again. "I will tell you nothing."

Heaving another painful sigh, Sakriel again holds his hand close to Hemlock's brand. Isiral and Orion keep a tight hold on him, pushing his shoulders back against the chair. Again the small man begins to writhe in pain. When Sakriel moves his hand even closer, almost touching the scaly patch, Hemlock cries out. Tears begin to coarse down the man's cheeks and his white-knuckled hands tangle themselves in his hair, wringing it until it comes from his scalp, drawing blood. Sakriel continues to fight his own inner sorrow for what he is being forced to do. He cannot not give in. The future of his world depends on the strength of them all, which means they must use any means possible to defeat the evil and end this.

As Hemlock continues to cry out, Sakriel lifts his eyes to Orion, then Isiral before moving them to the rest of the group, finally resting his gaze on Jara's face. In her eyes, and the rest, he finds understanding and acceptance. Each person understands what is at stake, and each is giving him their support. He finally looks down at Hemlock again, the small man suddenly crying out what Sakriel has been waiting to hear.

"I'll tell you! I'll tell you! Please, just stop! Please!"

Sakriel slowly closes his hand, moving it away. Walking

over to the table, he grabs a chair, placing it in front of Hemlock. He sits down and folds his strong arms across his chest. "All right, tell us."

Hemlock slowly sits up in the chair. Closing his robe, he runs a hand over his face, wiping away tears and sweat, leaving streaks of blood on his cheeks. He has been broken now, and he knows there is no turning back. He clears his throat, His voice raspy and hoarse when he speaks.

"As you already know, Ubal is planning to destroy the gateway back to the place of learning."

"Yes," Sakriel confirms. "Now we need to know how he plans to find the gate."

Hemlock hesitates before answering. "He is sending scouts out to find people who are at the end of their journey and are ready to go back."

"But that is impossible," Orion says. "Cillian speaks to a person's mind and tells him or her when they are ready. Ubal has never been able to master that ability. How could he know?"

"He doesn't," Hemlock says simply. "He has numerous followers and can spare enough to cover a great many people. Since there are very few left who have not been branded, he thinks his job will be fairly easy."

"So let me guess," Isiral says, his mouth twisting in a

wry smile. "Ubal plans to follow the person around and then jump them when the entrance appears. Does he not realize there are guards posted just inside the gate?"

"He does, however, he has informed me that there are ways around that problem."

"And just what are those ways?" Sakriel asks, leaning forward.

"He would not say."

"You mean you will not tell us," Orion states.

"No, I mean he would not say. He has revealed his plan, but not all the details, most of which he considers minor."

"No matter," Sakriel says. "He will fail."

"One more thing," Hemlock adds. "Take care and keep a watchful eye on your sister."

Isiral

Isiral's reflexes kick in and he yanks the small man up by the collar of his robe. "What is that supposed to mean?" When Sakriel places a calming hand on Isiral's shoulder, he drops the former guardian back into the chair. His emotions are running high at that moment and the thought of Ciran being in danger again is too much. Taking a calming breath, he steps back from the man.

Hemlock straightens his robe, looking up at the stormy expressions of all three men before addressing Sakriel.

"Ubal's hatred of your father runs deep as you already know. He is still determined to own your sister, only not just her soul but *her,* period. He knows that if he has her in his clutches, it will crush Cillian, making it that much easier for him to take over and destroy Krisandor."

Sakriel leans forward once more and says in an icy voice that chills the very room, "He will never get near her again, and he will never set foot in Krisandor. With everything in me, I will see him destroyed and his bones picked clean by the birds." He eyes the small man intently. "His followers will meet the same fate."

A subtle look of fear flits across Hemlocks face, and then the cold expression is back. "We shall see."

Isiral shakes his head at the man's insolence. It is obvious that Sakriel is finished with the man.

Sakriel stands. "Lema," he calls over his shoulder.

"Yes, Sakriel," one of the warriors answers, rising from the table.

"Get some rope to secure our prisoner."

The man immediately leaves on the errand.

"It does not matter what you do," Hemlock says, his face hard as stone. "You won't stop what is to be. Ubal will be victorious."

Ignoring Hemlock's remarks, Sakriel turns to the group.

"I will contact Father. Then we will plan."

Cillian

The large outdoor theater is completely filled. There isn't an empty bench. The announcement Cillian is about to make to the people concerns every citizen of Krisandor and all are in attendance. Young ones have been left at home at Cillian's request. His words are not for their ears.

Cillian looks out over the huge audience and ponders how much he loves each and every person here. He marvels anew at the growth of Krisandor and the goodness of the people. Love radiates throughout the whole land, the kind of love that breeds beauty, peace, and unconditional acceptance. He silently takes the sight in a moment longer, then he begins.

"My friends, my family, my brothers and sisters in the truest sense of the word. The announcement I am about to make is a most unpleasant one. Our kingdom, our beautiful home and our way of life, is being threatened. We are about to come under attack by evil. Ubal, the last dark lord of the other world is laying plans to enter our kingdom and destroy everything we have worked so hard to keep. We must not let this happen."

Cillian pauses a moment, allowing murmurs of shock and worry to die down. He lets his eyes sweep the anxious yet determined faces. When his gaze falls on the twelve leaders of the Inchant people, he smiles sadly. The Inchants have brought nothing but joy to Krisandor, and now they are involved in a war that *he* feels isn't theirs. But Emalon, the head of the leaders, with the support of his people has informed him that Krisandor is their home too, and it is their right and duty to help defend it. Cillian had to admit, he needs their strength and is grateful to count them among his people.

"The invading evil must not enter Krisandor," Cillian continues. "We must stop it before it even comes close. The only way to accomplish this is to leave Krisandor and fight Ubal and his followers in the other world." He stops and stands a moment in silence, allowing the citizens to fully grasp what is being asked of them. He sees the grief etched in their faces, but he also sees the determination and courage in their eyes, and in their countenances.

"Now I ask you, will you join me? Will you help me protect what is ours? Will you help me defeat Ubal?"

Immediately, a thunderous chorus of yeses ring throughout the land, every man and woman willing to sacrifice for their future and the future of their loved ones.

Cillian swallows hard against the emotion in his throat.

Now, it is time to ready his people.

Fourteen

Binding Hearts

A gentle breeze blows through my open window, tinkling the crystal chimes hanging from the top of the window frame. I slowly open my eyes as the beautiful music adds to the peacefulness of my surroundings. The previous events had exhausted me and this rest had been well needed. The sun is setting and an orange glow now bathes my room in a late afternoon ambiance.

I have only been awake for a few minutes when there is a gentle knock on my door. I sit up a little, pushing hair back from my face and straightening my robe. "Come in," I softly call. When the door opens, revealing Isiral timidly staring at me, my heart leaps. I did not expect it to be him. Just moments ago my dreams had been filled with him, and had been intensely real. But seeing him now draws forth feelings that completely overshadow the ones of my dreams. I smile shyly, smoothing a hand back over my hair again, a blush heating my cheeks.

Isiral

Isiral hesitates just inside the door, unsure if he should enter. However, as soon as the smile breaks across Ciran's beautiful face his heart melts.

"Please, come in," she says.

Isiral enters, closing the door. Ciran gestures to the chair by the window. He walks over and picks it up, placing it by her bed before sitting down. He watches her gracefully swing her legs off the bed and sit on the edge, facing him.

Both sit for a moment in silence and words hover at the tip of his tongue, he just has no idea what to say to her.

Isiral had come with the intent of telling her about the meeting, but now it is the furthest thing from his mind. Instead he asks, "Are you well?"

"I am better," Ciran answers.

For a moment he simply watches her watching him, and everything inside him longs to know her thoughts.

The man of my memories and dreams is here! He is really here before me, close enough to touch. And oh, how I long to touch him! He is everything I could have ever hope for and more. Everything inside me is crying out for him, longing for him to take me in his arms and hold me close to his heart. At this moment, not touching him is physically painful.

"Thank you," I finally manage to say, my hands tightening into fists. "Thank you for coming for me. It means more than I can possibly say."

Isiral

Isiral doesn't know how to respond, doesn't know how to fully express what is in his heart. How can he tell her of the ache inside him at the thought of her being harmed or in danger? How can he express the helpless and desperate love he feels for her, that he has felt for her longer than he can remember?

What can I say to you to express how much my very soul longs to reclaim you as my own? I can scarcely find the words.

What finally comes out is not what he had planned to say.

"You own my heart, fair Ciran. My very soul. How could I not come for you when my life's breath is so completely intertwined with yours?"

I stare at him, completely motionless, not daring to breathe. His words are poetry, the most beautiful poetry I have ever heard. In an instant, the memories that have been so distant are now at the forefront of my mind.

I remember him!

I really remember him! Every gentle angle of his face, the shimmering strands of his hair, his deep blue eyes, his rich voice. I remember the fullness of his mouth, the soft touch of his hand against my face, the rhythm of his heartbeat when I once rested my head against his chest, and the feel of his muscular arms around me. I remember walking with him, talking with him, sharing my thoughts and dreams with him.

How clearly I remember the look of love in his eyes when we shared our last moments together, and the pain in my own heart at the thought of being separated from him.

I remember everything.

Isiral catches the tear trailing down my cheek with his finger, his eyes registering the light of complete recognition in my own, and a joyous smile spreads across his face as tears spill. He slowly stands, our eyes intently locked. Holding his hands out to me, I stand also.

I say nothing, just simply continue to gaze up into his eyes, my every emotion written across my face. The feel of his large warm hands around her mine brings forth a sensation so new, yet so familiar. I ache to be closer still.

He gently laces her fingers between mine, slowly moving closer. My heart drums mercilessly as my eyes take in the yearning in his. Then he releases my hands, gently taking me in his arms and I am sure I will faint. Slowly, tenderly, gently, he rains kisses on my forehead, my eyes, my cheeks, and finally my lips. The sensation is as familiar to me as anything I have ever known.

I feel him sigh against my lips before deepening the kiss, every part of me melting against him. He holds me impossibly closer, and I never want to let him go, never want to be released from his arms.

After a moment he draws back slightly, looking into my eyes. "Will you take vows with me and complete our bonding?"

"I will," I answer without hesitation. I love him more than life itself. I always have.

Moving back a little more, he takes my hands in his. "We must inform Sakriel of our plans and have him perform the ceremony as soon as possible." A sudden shadow crosses his expression. "With war on our doorstep, there will be little time to prepare."

"I do not need to prepare," I tell him, squeezing his hands. "I have waited for this moment for a long time." I smile, my heart overflowing with love, the eternal kind that has no beginning or end. "I am ready."

"As am I." He touches my face, and then draws me back into his arms. "I love you," he whispers against my mouth, renewing his kiss, making up for time lost to us. Yet his kiss also holds the promise of forever. A promise we will move heaven and earth to keep.

Later in the evening as I get ready for bed, a permanent smile graces my face as my thoughts travel to Isiral. The man who has inhabited my memories and dreams has now proclaimed his love for me, and tomorrow morning we will be married. With all the despair facing us, never has a joyous occasion been needed more. And even the certainty of war with Ubal cannot dampen my joy.

I chuckle, remembering the smile that broke out across Sakriel's face when we shared our news with him. It was obvious he had already known who Isiral was to me. Orion had practically burst with happiness. Halia and Jara had embraced me and tearfully expressed their joy.

Heaving a contented sigh, I open my dresser and remove the crystal pendant. I ponder and meditate for a while before placing the precious and priceless possession back in its resting place. I am about to get into bed when there is a soft knock at the door. I can't help wondering who would be calling so late in the evening, and I am surprised when I open the door to Halia. Her smile is unsure.

"Please, come in," I say, smiling and moving aside.

"Thank you. I am sorry to come so late, but I needed to see you." Her smile widens. "I have something for you."

I watch the woman as she reaches into her robe pocket, pulling out the most beautiful bracelet I have ever seen.

Halia's smile turns melancholy. "This bracelet was given to me by someone very special. I want you to have it." She holds it out to me and I accept it, awe filling me.

"It is incredible! It is the most beautiful piece of jewelry I have ever seen." I examine it a moment. The bracelet is made of white gold and crystal beads are set between sections of gold. Small emeralds are mounted on the gold, and from the toggle clasp hangs a small, white-gold heart with a tiny emerald inserted in the middle.

"How can you bear to part with it?" I finally ask, amazed that she would give me such a gift.

Halia's eyes rests on the bracelet a moment before she raises her gaze to mine. "I wanted to give you something special, something that meant a great deal to me. I have treasured this bracelet above everything I own, and now I give it to you because you have come to mean even more." Her eyes slowly fill and she blinks the tears back quickly, swallowing hard before speaking again. Her voice is soft. "I will regret the things I have done for the rest of my life, but what I did to you will always hurt far more than any of my other deeds."

I tearfully look at the woman I first considered a friend, then an enemy, and now someone very dear to me.

"I hold nothing against you, Halia, and I am happy to be able to call you my friend."

"As am I," she says, touching my face. "Now," she said,

blinking back more tears, "I should let you get some sleep."

Nodding, I walk Halia to the door. "I am so glad you came to see me. And I don't know how to thank you for the beautiful bracelet."

"Seeing you wear it will be thanks enough." She squeezes my hand. "Goodnight, fair Ciran. Sleep well."

"You, too."

Fifteen

Love And Losses

A small circle of our closest friends are gathered in the grassy meadow behind Havenwood. Included in the group are Sakriel, Jara, Orion, Halia, and the five warriors who helped rescue me. All are dressed in their best robes in honor of this most sacred ceremony.

Facing each other with the naked light of undying love in our eyes, Isiral and I speak our vows. We are dressed in traditional wedding robes of white trimmed in silver and gold-twined rope. My hair hangs down my back and around my shoulders in dark, silky waves. A crown of white lilies wrapped in a strand of pearls and satin ribbon adorns my head. Isiral's golden locks are held in place at the back of his neck with a white silk tie. We are glowing in mutual adoration.

Because our father isn't here, the duty of choosing the bridal rings had fallen to Sakriel. He hands Isiral a diamond-cut gold band, instructing him to place it on my finger. I then place the matching band on Isiral's. Completing the ceremony, Sakriel wraps the ceremonial tie around our joined hands binding us to one another. Then we share our first kiss as husband and wife. We have now become one.

After a round of hugs and heart-felt congratulations and well wishes, we adjourn to the lower hall for a small celebration.

With war approaching, we decide it is best that we live at Havenwood instead of purchasing a home we will inevitably have to leave, for our time in this kingdom is fast approaching its end. Isiral settles up at Fairmoor and moves his belongings to my room. He and Sakriel also think it will be safer for me if we live here. Isiral doesn't want Ubal anywhere near me again and the risk would be too great anywhere else.

The next morning I awaken to find Isiral's side of the bed empty. I quickly sit up, briefly wondering if I dreamed the events of the day before. *What if none of it is real?* I shake my head, heaving a deep sigh.

Of course it was real! I lay back down, pressing my face into his pillow. Smiling, I snuggle into the covers. A moment later Isiral enters the room, carrying a breakfast tray.

"Good morning," I say. "I thought maybe I had dreamed the whole day yesterday."

Isiral smiles, placing the tray on the bed. "Never, my love. You are indeed my wife, and I am your husband."

"And I am more grateful than I can express."

He caresses my cheek a moment before leaning forward and kissing me. Drawing back, he places the tray over my lap.

"It truly was a wondrous day," I say. "More wonderful than I ever dreamed it would be."

"For me as well," he says softly, his smile wide. The look into his eyes quickly sobers. "You deserve so much more than this. If things were different . . ."

I softly touch a finger to his lips. "This is what we have. I have you, and I have your love. I need no more than that."

He leans forward, pressing his forehead to mine. "I am truly blessed," he whispers.

"As am I."

"So," he says as we begin eating our breakfast, "what would my wife like to do on her morning off?"

I smile, loving being referred to as his wife. "It does not matter. I have no preferences as long as we are together."

"No need to worry about that. I don't intend to let you out of my sight."

I teasingly quirk an eyebrow. "Is that because you cannot stand the thought of being away from me or is it merely a safety precaution?"

He grins. "Both, my love. However, my reasons tend to lean more toward the first."

"Good answer," I say and he laughs softly. "I guess that means you will be taking over Sakriel and Orion's job as my personal bodyguard."

"I will count myself blessed to be your protector."

"Protector," I murmur dreamily. "I like the sound of that." I sober a bit. "I am only sorry that I need protecting."

"Hey," Isiral says, touching my face. "You have nothing to be sorry for."

"I was told once that choice affects everything. I made a choice, and things happened because of that choice."

Isiral takes my face in his hands. "Listen to me, beloved. Yesterday has passed. You must let go and let it rest. The choices you have made since, as well as the ones you make now are the choices that are important. As for what is happening, you have nothing to do with it. This quickly-spreading evil is Ubal's doing and the vengeance he harbors existed long before you were born. And it will continue until we end this." He pauses, caressing my face. "Let it go, my Ciran. Let it go."

Closing my eyes, I rest my forehead to his as fresh tears trail down my cheeks. "I will try," I whisper. Moving back slightly, I muster enough courage to draw forth a smile. "All right, no more sadness. I will not mar what precious time we have with regrets."

Isiral kisses me. "Then we shall savor every moment of the present."

I nod and quietly stare into his eyes a moment, a thousand feelings and emotions flowing through me, yet mere words cannot express what is in my heart. Three must suffice.

"I love you."

"And I love you."

After surrendering to each other's arms awhile longer, we eat our breakfast and discuss our plans for the day. We are just finishing when there is a loud knock at the door.

"I will get it," Isiral says, getting up.

"Isiral," Jara says, slightly frantic. "There is an emergency meeting in the lower hall. They need you to come right now. I am to stay here with Ciran."

I immediately jump out of bed, rushing to Isiral's side. "What has happened?"

"We just received word that Ubal and some of his followers are on their way to Havenwood. Sakriel wants us to remain here. It will be safer."

I squeeze Isiral's arm, my concern and fear renewed.

Isiral draws me into his arms. "I must go down, but do not worry." He leans down, kissing me softly. "Lock the door behind me," he whispers against my lips, holding me tightly for a moment longer before releasing me and leaving the room.

Halia

Halia discreetly follows the slender shrouded figure down the dimly-lit abandoned corridor. Every now and then the intruder glances behind him, and each time, Halia manages to find something to hide behind. This time when he looks back, she quickly ducks behind a large statue and takes a deep breath, trying to slow her racing heart, acutely aware of beads of perspiration trailing down her temples. She senses the person is a danger to Ciran and needs to be stopped before he can reach her. Sakriel and the others are occupied in their own fight at the moment.

Firmly curling her fingers around the handle of the dagger hidden in the deep pocket of her gown, Halia quietly proceeds with caution. Reaching the end of the corridor, the intruder turns left and Halia slows her step, growing even more cautious. She stands silently for a moment, waiting before turning the corner.

She hadn't waited long enough.

Halia's eyes widen in shock as the dagger, appearing from nowhere, pierces her chest. She falls to the floor in a heap, but only after stabbing the assailant in the side with her own weapon.

In an instant, all the poor choices she has made in her life are placed before her. She also glimpses the choices she should have made but didn't, and the consequences they wrought.

As she lay watching the cloaked figure slowly limping away, she is surprised to see each of her mistakes vanish as well.

I am startled by a soft knock on the door.

"Who is it?" I ask.

"It is Enya."

This takes me by complete surprise. It has been too long since Enya last spoke to me. I open the door.

"Ciran, you and Jara must come with me now! I have to get you out of here before Ubal comes."

I take in Enya's frantic expression. "Why are you warning us?"

"Because," she says quickly, glancing down the hall. "I may have chosen a different path from yours, but I do not want to see you harmed."

I am frightened but still skeptical. Jara lends voice to my thoughts.

"Sakriel told us to remain here and that is what we will do."

"I am trying to help you," Enya hisses. "You must go!"

"Thank you for your help," I tell her, "but we will stay and wait for our husbands to come."

"Your husbands will be dead soon, as will you if you do

not listen to me."

"We will stay here," I repeat, sensing that something isn't right about Enya's willingness to help us. I move to close the door when a large hand appears from nowhere, shoving the door wide open.

"Kundar!" I cry, my heart racing in shock.

"I told you they wouldn't cooperate," he says to Enya as he pushes his way into the room.

I grab Jara's hand, backing away from him.

"Let's not make this harder than it has to be, Ciran," he says, smiling, inching closer. "Ubal is waiting for his prize and I intend to deliver his prize to him even if I have to knock you out to do it." He grins at Jara. "And you, my dear, will be an added bonus."

Jara squeezes my hand hard, causing me to wince slightly. I can feel her fear even more than my own. I boldly look from Kundar to Enya, and then back at Kundar. "We will not go with you."

Enya and Kundar laugh. "Is that so?" he asks, amusement in his voice. "We will see about that."

Kundar moves to grab me. Releasing Jara's hand, I back toward the dresser and pick up the large crystal vase of flowers, throwing it at him. Kundar quickly ducks and the vase hits Enya instead, shattering upon contact. The girl immediately drops to her knees, holding her head. Kundar briefly glances at her before turning his rage-filled eyes back to me.

"Oh, you will pay for that."

He lunges at me, catching my wrist. I try to pull away, but his grip is solid. He yanks me forward, pinning both of my arms behind my back. Behind him, I watch Jara pick up a thick book, but it is apparent he notices as well. Holding me to him with one arm, his other hand shoots out and catches Jara's arm before she can hit him with it. He squeezes her wrist tightly, causing her to cry out and she drops the book. Then with lightening speed, he slams a fist against the side of her face. She crumbles to the floor.

Enraged, I begin kicking and writhing my body wildly, fighting against him with everything I have.

"You know what? I am growing weary of this," Kundar says before brutally butting his head against mine. The blinding pain produces stars before my eyes and my legs give beneath me. I try to get up, but the pain makes it impossible. Tears seep from my closed eyes as Kundar's amused voice echoes in my ears.

"Well," he says to Enya, "that was easy, was it not?"

I open my my eyes, watching Enya smile back through her own obvious pain. "Yes, I daresay it was."

Yanking me with him, Kundar grabs a rope from the hallway while Enya keeps a close eye on Jara.

"Keep watching that one," he says, gesturing to Jara as he ties my hands.

No, not again! my mind screams as my arms are bound behind my back. A large, lump has formed on my left temple. My thoughts go to Jara where she lay and I pray my sister-in-law is all right. *Isiral*, I plead inwardly, *please come back*. I again close my eyes against the pain. *I need you.*

After Kundar is finished tying my ankles together, he binds Jara. He is just finishing when the room door is violently kicked open. Isiral stands in the doorway, his chest and shoulders heaving in rage. In the next instant, he has the collar of Kundar's robe in his hands and is pounding his face repeatedly until the man is unconscious. He turns as Enya backs away through the door, but she is stopped by an equally angry Sakriel. He hands her to Elan, one of the unbranded warriors, instructing him to place her with the other two men still alive.

Isiral drops to his knees and unties me. Picking me up, he cradles me against his chest and I soak in his comforting strength.

"I am so sorry," he whispers against my ear as I cling to him. "I am so sorry."

"It was not your fault," I tell him, burying my face against his neck.

Sakriel stands, cradling Jara in his arms and turns to Isiral. "We must leave and take them to the safe place. Things have gotten too dangerous and we cannot wait any longer." He turns as Kingi, another young warrior, appeared in the doorway.

"Take Kundar and and lock him up with the others," Sakriel instructs him. "You know where to meet us afterward. Take care that you are not followed."

Kingi nods, picking up an unconscious Kundar, slinging him over his shoulder.

"Can you walk, beloved?" Isiral softly asks me. I nod and he gently lowers me to my feet.

"Sakriel."

We all turn at the sound of Gensal's voice. The tall warrior stands in the doorway holding the injured body of Halia.

"I found her in a corridor of the west wing."

"Oh, Halia," I whisper brokenly. She is covered in blood, her face pale.

Sakriel gently places Jara in a chair and instructs Gensal to lay Halia on the bed. He kneels beside her.

Halia slowly opens her eyes. Her breathing is shallow.

She smiles weakly. "My journey has finally come to its sad end," she says, her voice breaking. "Now you must leave me here and go."

Sakriel takes her hand in his, squeezing it gently. "Not so sad in the end," he says. The emotion in his voice is thicker than I have ever heard it. "It is your time, I know, but in the end you were true to your heart." He presses his free hand to her cheek. "Each of us has a purpose, a reason for being here, and yours is clear. You helped to protect something very precious to us both."

Halia releases a weak sob. "Where is Ciran?"

Sakriel glances up at me where I stand in the circle of Isiral's arms, tears streaking my face. Isiral releases me and I join my brother at her side.

I study the fatal stab wound in Halia's chest and heave a bitter sob. I have grown to love her more than I ever imagined I could and the thought of losing her is unbearable.

"Forgive me," Halia rasps, her voice growing weaker.

"You have already been forgiven," I tell her, trying to smile.

"No," Halia says, raising her eyes to Sakriel. "Forgive me for being weak. For not being there for you, for betraying you, and . . . your father."

Stunned, my eyes jump to Sakriel's, then Halia's, and

finally Sakriel's again, the sudden dawning of truth taking hold. I continue to stare into my brother's eyes, finding confirmation in his tear-filled gaze.

Never moving his eyes from mine, he says, "All is forgiven, Mother."

The soft gasps from Isiral, Jara, and Gensal are heard but ignored, for we are momentarily in a world of their own.

A menagerie of emotions flicker through me, racing through my heart–emotions that cannot be put into words, but the end feeling is peace. For this brief moment I have my mother. I will not waste these final seconds harboring anger or regret. I will use it in the only way I know how.

"I love you, Mother. Go, and be at peace."

Sixteen

The Way Of Things

As we ride in the carriage, Isiral continues to hold me, drying my tears, sharing my pain. After all the years of wondering, I finally met my mother. It had been brief, but the time I was able to spend with her was priceless.

I continue swallowing against the pain. My mother is at peace now, but oh, how I will miss her! I did not have enough time with her, and part of that time I had considered her my enemy. How grateful I am now that I hadn't known Halia was my mother then. And yet . . .

Shaking my head slightly, I alter the direction of my thoughts. I will have no regrets, and will only remember our last days together and treasure them. My thoughts drift to Sakriel. He has known all along who Halia was, yet he never said a word. I suppose it had been for the best.

I wince slightly as Isiral gently presses a cool cloth over the lump on my temple. Lying back in my husband's arms on the soft pallet that will be our bed for the next while, I sigh as the coolness of the cloth relieves some of the pain. Opening my eyes, I allow my gaze to travel around the torch-lit cavern. Sakriel and Orion prepared the chambers of this hidden cave last week, not knowing it would be needed sooner than expected.

The red stone walls and ceiling are jagged in some spots, and each wall holds a torch, which sits in a snugly-carved hole. The ground is covered in soft animal skin, the pine borough pallet topped with a thick down-filled cushion, covered by a soft warm blanket. The fire pit in the middle of the cavern fills our surroundings with warmth.

"How are you feeling?" Isiral asks, holding the cloth to my head.

"Better," I answer with a tired sigh. I shift my head slightly, wanting to look at him. "I should not have opened the door. I am sorry."

"Do not be sorry, beloved. It is I who should apologize. I should have come back sooner."

Reaching up, I press a hand against his cheek. "You could not have known. And I daresay you were busy in a fight of your own."

He heaves a tired sigh. "Still, I should be able to keep you safe." He places a finger under my chin, his gaze intent. "I promise you, I *will* protect you from now on." He smiles. "You are everything to me, and I would not be able to exist in Krisandor–*if* there is a Krisandor left after all of this– without you."

"Nor I you," I whisper, drawing his head down, kissing him warmly. "Nor I you."

Sakriel

Sitting in the cavern he would share with Jara, Sakriel heaves a deep sigh and opens his eyes, letting the words he'd just received from his father comfort him and buoy him up for what is to come. He must tell everyone. There is only one more day to prepare. One more day to search Jubilus for any unbranded souls. One more day to reach those people who wish to be *unbranded*. One more day until the fates of the two worlds will be decided.

"All will be well, my love," Jara says, clearly sensing the unrest lying beneath the surface. She wraps her arms around him, resting her head against his shoulder.

Sakriel sighs, burying his face in her hair. Pulling her into himself, he relishes the warmth of her embrace. "I know," he finally responds. "I know that eventually all will be made right. One way or another."

Ubal looks up from his evening meal, taking in Kundar and Enya's disheveled appearance. "What do you mean you couldn't get her?" he roars upon hearing Kundar's report.

Kundar feels Enya flinch beside him. Wincing against the pain of his swollen jaw, he looks steadily into the evil eyes of the dark lord. "Sakriel had others there with him. We had not anticipated that and were outnumbered."

Ubal pops a grape in his mouth. "So in other words, you failed." His eyes burn into Kundar. "Do you realize that having Ciran in my possession would have been my surety of breaking my enemy? And since my other little rat's ears have not returned to me, I have no doubt they know our plan now, so I will have to change our course of action. I was counting on having her."

"But we don't need her to win. You have many followers, more than enough to crush their pitiful band. And once we destroy the gate, they will be powerless to stop us from taking over."

Ubal flashes a dark smile. "How true, how true." He takes a long drink of Splendorfire. Placing the goblet on the table, he says, "Gather everyone together for the final preparations. Tomorrow at dawn we will strike. Cillian and his people will never know what hit them."

Sakriel

Sakriel exhausts himself as he and the other men travel about throughout the evening, making one last effort to try and share the truth of Ubal's treachery with others. While most shun them and turn a deaf ear, a few listen and believe, and Sakriel is able to use his gift to heal them, making them fair once again. He then tells them where to gather, preparing them the best he can. Of course, he understands no amount of preparation will suffice for what is to come. Still, he and the others do what they can. As for those who will not make a choice one way or the other, after tonight, the choice will be made for them.

Wrapped in Isiral's arms, we stand outside the entrance of the cave. I soak in the warm comfort of his muscular embrace and silently gaze up at the hazy moon. The tension in the air is tangibly thick, the time of any semblance of peace having long since passed. I turn, burrowing deeper in his embrace and he tightens his arms around me, securing me in a blanket of protection and love.

We find words completely unnecessary, so rather than disturb what might be our last peaceful moments in this life, we speak to each other with our hearts, with our eyes, and with our very souls.

By the deep dark of night, seven cloaked figures approach the secret entrance of the cave and a tall form exits. Flanked on either side by the six, the leader moves forward, lifting the hood of his cape, and the two men embrace.

"Come, Father," Sakriel says, his voice filled with

emotion. "She is inside."

Isiral is sitting with his back against the wall, deep in thought, idly running gentle fingers through his sleeping wife's hair, her head cradled in his lap, when Cillian enters their torch-lit chamber. Isiral looks up and is greeted by the familiar loving smile he has so missed.

Cillian

Cillian quietly lowers himself to the pallet, and for a moment, just watches his beautiful daughter sleep. How he has missed her! How he has ached to see her again, to hold her safely against his heart and know beyond a doubt she is all right. Now, here she is before him, and he is suddenly afraid to awaken her, afraid she will not remember him. Deep inside he knows this is utter nonsense, but a part of him is afraid just the same. It has been so long, yet it hasn't. It's been over two years since she left Krisandor to start her journey, yet it seems like only yesterday that he had said goodbye to his precious daughter.

After another moment, Cillian timidly reaches out and takes her hand in his, holding his breath as her eyes slowly open.

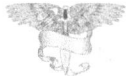

I smile at the face before me, thinking it is my brother. Then I blink and the face comes completely into focus. When it does, tears quickly fill my eyes, for I know this man as surely as I know my own name. I sit up, my bottom lip trembling.

"Father," is all I manage to say, and in the next instant, my face is buried in the folds of his robe.

"Yes, my angel," he whispers, wrapping me in his warm embrace.

"Oh, Father, Father, Father," I repeat over and over again.

"I am here, my angel. I am here, and I have missed you so."

"And I have missed you," I sob. "So much."

"I know," he soothes. "It will all be over soon." He draws back, smoothing the hair from my face.

"I remember everything now," I say, looking into his kind, loving eyes. "I remember you, my home, my friends, everything."

Father's smile is rueful, and one that I remember well.

"Part of me worried that you would not. It was foolish, I know, but I worried just the same."

I give him a watery smile. "Oh, Father."

He softly caresses my face. "We must get you back to Krisandor and settle you safely in the palace. The days of traditional re-entry have ended."

I wipe my face. "I am so sorry, Father."

"Do not be," he says with a sad smile.

Looking into his eyes, I hesitate before asking, "You know about Mother?"

He nods, again caressing my cheek. "I know."

"In the end she made the right choice."

"I know that, too. I am only sad you did not have more time with her when that time really counted."

"It was enough," I say. "In the end she waged her own war with Ubal and won."

"It was to be," Father says with a sigh. "So it must be with us all. It is the way of things. Good and evil cannot coexist forever."

He pauses, turning to Sakriel. I take in the look of mutual love and understanding passing between the two. "Whether it be the loss of my life or that of my enemy, tomorrow we must end this."

Seventeen

Vindication

The dawning of the following day is one that will be written in the history books. It will be a story told for generations to come.

Ubal and thousands upon thousands of his followers trudge down the four streets leading to the town square. The sound of numberless footsteps echoes against the vast surroundings, their voices raised in the cry of war. Both men and women are dressed in leather leggings, rough-spun tunics and boots. They carry swords, shields, daggers, and slings. Their faces are painted, some only partially, the rest completely. They wear the look of evil in their eyes and carry murderous intentions in their hearts.

The sky is gray and overcast, and not a living thing stirs. It is as if all of nature is holding its breath in silent anticipation of what is to come.

A half a mile from the square, the men and women begin to chant, their steps quickening.

Death to Krisandor, new life to Jubilus.
In darkness there is power, in Ubal there is life.

Ubal

Ubal smiles as the chant rings throughout the land. This is the day he was born for, the moment he was born for. This is his time. He is about to lay claim to what is rightfully his. He will have absolute power. Power over everything and everyone. Before this day is done he will see Cillian bow down to him.

Yes, today is his day.

He and his followers continue their march, anticipating certain victory. However, Ubal's countenance quickly changes when they reach the entrance of the square. All of his minions freeze and absolute silence comes over them. Ubal blinks, shocked by what his eyes now behold.

The town square is completely full. Faces without number stretching back beyond the gateway as far as the eye can see, stare back at him and his followers.

Humans, guardians, Inchants. All of them are standing side by side in unity. At the forefront of the mass stand Sakriel, Orion, Isiral, and Elan.

And at the head of these warriors stands Cillian.

The arrogant smile that had only seconds ago graced Ubal's face is gone, and in its place is a look of rage, drawn forth by the realization that his easy victory has been stolen from his grasp.

Cillian

Cillian faces Ubal in stony silence, fully understanding that this is the end. There is no turning back now. The time for negotiation has passed. The friendship they once shared is completely dead, never to be revived. One or both of them will die today.

No words of peace are offered. No pleas of supplication are spoken. There would be no point.

If Cillian feels anything, it is sorrow for the lives that will be lost. Sorrow for those who have chosen to stay loyal to Ubal. Sorrow for those who made no choice at all. Sorrow for what could have been. Sorrow for the ones whose eyes have now been opened only to discover that it is too late to turn back.

Other than burning hatred, he senses nothing from Ubal. Absolutely nothing.

Alas, the stage is set at this final hour.

The Krisandorians advance, taking Ubal and his followers by surprise. Soon the sounds and smells of war fill the air; the clashing of swords, the pounding of axes against metal shields, the swish of poisonous darts fired from Inchant blowguns, and arrows launched from their bows. The tearing of flesh, the scent of blood and sweat. All are thick in the air.

The earth groans and cracks beneath their feet, experiencing a pain of its own as the evil begins to be purged from its system. Like a body trying to fight off a long-suffered sickness, the land had grown weak is now regenerating in strength as new life slowly infuses it.

Cillian matches Ubal's sword stroke for stroke, blow for blow, never a pause or a moment of rest in between. Ubal quickens his brutal pace and Cillian matches it without taking a breath. Each has their eye fixed on the other, waiting for the precise moment to execute the final blow.

Then it comes.

From the garden room inside the palace, we painfully listen to the distant cries of war. The shouts of anger, pain and anguish echo throughout the land, and the sound is impossible to block out. The women and children of Krisandor are locked in our homes, sheltered from the scenes of carnage.

All of us were waiting–waiting to know our fate.

Waiting to know the fate of those we love.

My head rests against Mazina's shoulder and the beautiful Inchant caresses my hair, softly crooning words of comfort in her own native tongue. Jara and Maylee are also here, holding hands and doing their best to comfort one another. We are all in danger of losing the men we love and are doing our best to be strong.

However, we understand with absolute clarity what is at stake. Krisandor is our home, *our* kingdom. And it is worth fighting for.

It is worth sacrificing for, and worth dying for.

It is worth everything.

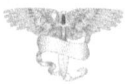

The fighting lasts for the better part of the morning. In the end, the Krisandorians suffer a fair amount of injuries but no casualties. However, the streets are littered with the blood and bodies of their enemies.

Sakriel pulls his sword from the chest of the last man he killed, wiping the blade clean. He stands scanning the area for his father, momentarily taking in the survivors. Clothes and faces are streaked with blood. Eyes are full of sadness, misery, woe, and gladness that it is over.

When Sakriel finally spots Cillian's body slumped over another in the distance, his eyes cloud. Dropping his sword, he runs to him. As Sakriel draws near, he realizes his father is still alive, and he is weeping. He kneels beside him, taking his father's shoulders in his hands.

Cillian raises up, uninjured, and looks down at the man who was once his brother.

Sakriel puts an arm around his father. "You had no choice, Father. It had to be done."

Cillian sighs. "I know, son. I know." He lets his eyes slowly travel over the grizzly sight before looking toward the palace in the distance. "Your sister and wife, and Maylee?" he suddenly inquires.

"They are safe, Father," Sakriel assures him. "We made sure no one got through."

Settling his gaze on Ubal's face a final time, Cillian stands.

"It is finished, son. Let us go home."

Epilogue

Day Of Peace

The moon is full and stars twinkle brightly in the clear sky. Taking it all in, I rest on a granite bench in the palace courtyard, my back against Isiral's chest, wrapped securely in his arms. I can't help smiling as I continue to gaze up at the heavens, my hand lightly pressed against Isiral's where it lay on my round abdomen. I revel in the peace and contentment filling me from being home again.

Humming softly, the gentle strains of my voice rustles the leaves on the trees, causing them to answer back. My gift upon returning had been the gift of an angel's voice, and amazingly, every time I open my mouth, the very elements obey my command. Any and everyone I speak with walks away with a feeling of calmness. The ability will never cease to leave me in awe.

It has been a year since the final war took place that sealed the gate of Krisandor forever, and that year has been one of renewed gratitude and hope for the future.

I feel that hope and gratitude every time our little one moves inside me. The promise of new life always brings a sense of peace, and each time I gaze into my husband's eyes, the sensation is renewed. It seems like only yesterday that I said goodbye to him at the gate to begin my journey, not years ago. Now here we are. He had found me, and blessedly, I had been worthy of him.

How grateful I am to have had the experiences I did, and for the knowledge I gained through them. It is a gift I will treasure always.

Choice.

It is a fickle thing, this word choice. For upon this word sits all others. Upon this act sits every consequence. Upon this act is the vast and unknown fate of all things decided.

Pondering this truth, I smile.

My father had been right, though. The journey had been worth it, and I am now blessed with all I could ever want.

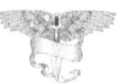

But alas, contrary to popular belief, all is not yet right with the world.

About The Author

When J. (Jewel) Adams was a teenager, the last thing she ever thought she would be doing when she grew up was writing books. She wrote a lot of poetry in high school, but writing full-fledged novels was definitely a surprise to her. She finished her first book in 1996 and hasn't stopped yet.

Mainly authoring romantic fiction, she decided it was time to go in a slightly different direction–young adult romantic fantasy with a message.

Jewel is the author of several published novels and ebooks, and is a motivational speaker. She and her husband, Sean, are the parents of eight children and reside in West Point, Utah.

You can email Jewel at jewela40@gmail.com

She loves hearing from her readers!

To purchase other books by J. Adams, visit her website at J Adams Novels. Also, log onto her her blog at jewelsbestgems.blogspot.com

J. Adams